"Knock, knock." Jessa [...] in the room.

Clint stared at her as she walked in. What had happened to the cute little freckle-faced redhead with wild hair and up-turned nose?

In her place stood a vision of beauty. Her strawberry-blond hair was twisted up with some kind of clip, and curls cascaded down from it. He couldn't tell she had on any makeup, but she must have, because the freckles were nowhere to be seen. And something she'd done made her eyes stand out until he thought he could get lost in them.

"Breathe, Son," his dad muttered in his ear.

"Jessa, come in." Elaine grinned at Jeb's barely perceptible comment but hurried over to make her guest feel at home.

"Is there anything I can do to help?"

"Well, let's see. . ." Elaine wiped her hands on the towel that hung on the cabinet pull and nodded. "You can put the ice in the glasses."

While she got Jessa started on her assigned task, Clint inwardly thanked his mom for giving him time to gather his thoughts.

"So, Clint?" Jessa asked over her shoulder as she divvied ice cubes into the glasses, "Did you recognize me without the ponytail?"

He grinned. Trust her to address his speechlessness head on. "You clean up real nice."

"Thanks." She turned back to Elaine. "Nothing like begging for a compliment."

Clint smiled politely, but his pulse pounded in his ears. His career was over, his life in turmoil, his faith a wreck. Now was the worst possible time for him to meet the girl of his dreams. But his heart seemed to have a mind of its own.

CHRISTINE LYNXWILER and her husband, Kevin, live in the foothills of the beautiful Ozark Mountains in their home state of Arkansas. Christine's greatest earthly joy is her family, and aside from God's work, spending time with them is her top priority.

Books by Christine Lynxwiler

HEARTSONG PRESENTS
HP 526—In Search of Love
HP 549—Patchwork and Politics

Don't miss out on any of our super romances. Write to us at the following address for information on our newest releases and club information.

Heartsong Presents Readers' Service
PO Box 719
Uhrichsville, OH 44683

Or visit www.heartsongpresents.com

Through the Fire

Christine Lynxwiler

Heartsong Presents

Dedicated to my incredible mom, Ermyl Elaine McFadden Pearle.

Also to the rest of my wonderful family, too numerous to name here, but you know who you are! (This includes my brother, Kenny Pearle, who is positive I'll never dedicate a book to him, even though he's the very best brother in the world.) Thank you all!

As always, thanks to my fantastic husband, Kevin, and the most precious two daughters anyone could ever have.

A huge thank you to my Father in heaven who makes each day possible.

Grateful acknowledgment to Don Morgan and his buddies at the Cherokee Village Fire Department for sharing their expertise. Any mistakes are mine alone.

A note from the Author:
I love to hear from my readers! You may correspond with me by writing:

Christine Lynxwiler
Author Relations
PO Box 719
Uhrichsville, OH 44683

ISBN 1-59310-240-2

THROUGH THE FIRE

Our mission is to publish and distribute inspirational products offering exceptional value and biblical encouragement to the masses.

All Scripture quotations are taken from the King James Version of the Bible.

All of the characters and events in this book are fictitious. Any resemblance to actual persons, living or dead, or to actual events is purely coincidental.

PRINTED IN THE U.S.A.

Or check out our Web site at www.heartsongpresents.com

prologue

"You sure about this, Clint?" The gray-haired man behind the desk regarded him with solemn eyes.

Not trusting himself to speak, Clint McFadden nodded. He gently laid his firefighter badge on the scarred surface of the desk.

The older man picked up the shiny object and rubbed his thumb over it. "I know losing Ryan was rough on you. It was hard on the whole department." He cleared his throat and looked back up at Clint. "But it happens in this business. We have to go on. It's our job."

He met the probing gaze of his boss and knew that if he didn't explain, Steve would keep trying to change his mind. As he searched for the right words, images jumped through his brain like a video stuck on fast-forward.

Flames. Deadly, leaping flames. The crackle of his radio— "Ryan's still inside." Running through the burning building, fueled by the driving hope of getting to his best friend. Then, his pounding heart as he faced the murderous wall of fire between him and Ryan. Finally, the bottomless agony of knowing there was no passage through. If only. . .

"It's—" His voice broke. He bowed his head, unwilling for his crusty old boss to see the tears that edged his eyes.

"It's terrible, that's what it is. But it happens. We don't need to lose another good fireman." Compassion rang in the older man's voice. Clint raised his head.

Moisture glistened in Steve's eyes, looking out of place in

his weather-beaten face. "There's no shame in grieving a friend. But you know he'd want you to go on."

He shook his head. "Not if he knew how I felt."

Steve pushed back from the desk and came around to put his hand on Clint's shoulder. "How about just taking some time off? It's only been a week since the fire. Maybe a vacation would give you a new perspective."

Frustration made Clint's words come out more clipped than he intended. "No, it's better to just be done with it. You can fill my position, and I'll find another job."

"You're giving up firefighting completely?" Steve's tone was incredulous.

"I have to."

"Why?"

A mantle of humiliation and despair settled on Clint's shoulders as he whispered the words he knew Steve would have no choice but to accept. "I'm afraid to go back into another fire."

one

Jessa Sykes wasn't sure if the fragrance of past bouquets really lingered in the air of the small shop or if it was her excited imagination. She looked around, hardly noticing the bare shelves and empty refrigerated coolers. Instead, her mind's eye pictured rows of cut flowers and vibrant silk arrangements. "It's going to be perfect!"

Evelyn's short gray bob bounced as she nodded. "I knew it was just what you were looking for. Ruby has always loved it." Her mouth tightened. "She hates to give it up." The sober expression gave way to a smile. "But she'll be glad to see young blood keeping her dream alive."

Jessa ran her hand along the cool cream-swirled marble counter and glanced up at Evelyn. From the time Jessa had been a little tot begging cookies from her doting, childless, next-door neighbor, the two had established a relationship based on honesty and frankness. "Regrets?" she asked softly.

Evelyn chuckled. "Plenty." She winked. "Oh, you mean about convincing Ruby to sell you her shop? Not really."

"Has it been terribly hard on her?" Jessa knew Evelyn's sister had put her heart and soul into the business she'd grown from scratch thirty years ago.

Ruby had closed the flower shop only weeks before when her failing health had made it necessary for Evelyn to move back to Arkansas from Georgia to help care for her. Now the two sisters lived together in an assisted living center less than a block away.

"No. She knew it was more than she could handle." She looked thoughtful. "As a matter of fact, Ruby and I had been praying about what she would do with The Flower Basket right before you called that night from Georgia and told me you were quitting your job. When you said you wanted to open up your own flower shop far away from Atlanta, I had no doubt it was the answer to our prayers." Evelyn shook her head. "No, no regrets on that front."

"On that front, huh? That must mean you've heard from Mom." Jessa sank into one of the two folding chairs that constituted the only furniture in the building.

"She called." Evelyn smiled softly and sat opposite her. "She can't help but worry. You're her baby."

"I'm well aware of that, Auntie Ev. I'm everybody's baby!"

"Not anymore." The older woman shook her head again. "A baby wouldn't be here, about to open her very own business, five hundred miles from home."

"That's what I'm counting on. But that doesn't keep them from calling just to see for themselves that I'm all right."

"What do you tell them?" The intuitiveness in Evelyn's eyes bore into Jessa's soul, and she ducked her head.

"Most of the time I let the automated message answer." Jessa had jumped at the chance to relocate and reinvent herself, not giving her parents or sister a chance to protest, at least not in person. She knew they loved her, but their constant fretting did nothing for her self-confidence.

"I guess it's natural that they're worried then." There was no condemnation in Evelyn's tone. Just a quiet understanding of both sides.

The memory of her family's disapproval of the new venture came to mind, and the flowery fragrance Jessa had imagined earlier dissipated. In its place hovered a closed-up, musty smell. She suddenly saw clearly all the things that could go wrong. "I know it's natural, and I promise I'll try harder to keep in touch with them."

She regarded the woman who had always supported her. Unlike her family, Evelyn never said "That's too dangerous," which Jessa knew meant, "That's too dangerous *for you*, Jessa." The older woman was probably the only person in her life who didn't think Jessa still needed help tying her shoes at twenty-six. "But, you have to promise me something."

"What's that?"

"Promise no matter how things go here—good or bad— you won't tell my family."

The older woman pursed her lips and glanced toward the ceiling as if considering Jessa's request, then grinned, looking far younger than retirement age. "You've got a deal."

After they shared a laugh and shook hands to seal the agreement, Jessa softly spoke. "Thanks."

"No problem. I'd already decided not to be their informant."

"No, I mean, thanks for taking a chance on me." She knew that if Evelyn hadn't financed half the purchase price, the bank wouldn't have been nearly as cooperative as they had been, agreeing to finance the other half plus initial invest- ment money at a low interest. "If it weren't for you. . ."

Evelyn waved her hand in dismissal. "If it weren't me, it would have been somebody else—if this is God's plan for you. As much as you're dying to be in charge of your own life, hon, you're not." She smiled and pointed heavenward. Jessa recognized the teasing glint in her eyes. "You'll always be His baby."

"I'm fine with that." Jessa returned her grin. "At least He lets me make my own choices." She grimaced. "Even if they're not always the greatest."

Evelyn cleared her throat. "Speaking of making your own choices, have you given any more thought to whether you'll be able to keep Doris on? I hate to ask, but Ruby's really worried about her. Last we heard she hadn't found a job." Evelyn rushed on, and her face turned a little red. "If you can't, I understand."

"Actually, I think I'll be able to use my savings to pay her wages until The Flower Basket can afford to. She's familiar with the business, and I know she was a loyal assistant to Ruby." Jessa smiled as she envisioned the now-empty building bustling with activity and brimming with customers. "If the business gets going again right away, like I'm praying it will, I should have no problem keeping her on or paying Seth to do deliveries. I'm going to call them both this afternoon."

"Wonderful." Evelyn stood. "I'd better get back to the apartment and tell Ruby. She'll be so happy."

Jessa pushed to her feet and gave the older woman a hug. "Thanks again."

As the door closed behind her friend, Jessa turned back and ran her hand along the counter again. Just a few more days and, Lord willing, this shop would be filled with customers, and she and Doris would keep sixteen-year-old Seth busy making deliveries. Reality faded away again, and she immersed herself for a few luxurious moments in the make-believe garden of flowers and beauty and dreams come true.

When the tinkling bell over the front door sounded, she pivoted, prepared to tease her old friend about forgetting something. But, instead of the petite, gray-haired woman she expected, a tall, blond man loomed in the doorway. His blue eyes widened as he glanced around the bare store.

"Am I in the wrong place?" He leaned back out the door and peered at the painted words on the window. "It still says

THE FLOWER BASKET. Did Ruby move?"

"Actually, she retired." Jessa smoothed down her T-shirt over her faded jeans and tried not to think about what she must look like. She hadn't planned on seeing anyone today, certainly not a handsome stranger. And in spite of his unshaven face and brooding eyes, this stranger was the epitome of handsome. "I bought the shop a week ago. It won't reopen for a few days, though. I'm sorry."

He nodded and flashed a rueful grin. "That's okay. My mom loves flowers, and I thought that maybe an unusual bouquet would help distract her attention from the return of her prodigal son. . .stave off a few questions. . ." He murmured the last words so softly Jessa had to strain to hear them. "Guess I'll have to think of something else." He offered her a crooked smile, but the returning sadness in his eyes grabbed at Jessa's heartstrings.

"I'm sorry," she repeated, uncertain why her knees felt weak. She'd never been prone to "like" at first sight. But there was something about this man. His vulnerability, perhaps. Or maybe just the hide-and-seek dimples.

"Not a problem, really."

"The Grand Opening celebration begins next week."

"Okay, thanks. I'll be back." Without another word, he nodded and exited the store.

She stood staring at the tiny bell that still jangled to and fro above the doorjamb. She had the feeling there was much more to her mystery man than met the eye.

❧

Clint McFadden woke with a start, violently pushing against the blanket that seemed to smother and strangle him. Finally rid of the offending cover, he leaped to his feet, blinking against the inky darkness. Where was he?

He forced himself to take deep, slow breaths—pulling air in through his nose, blowing out through his mouth by instinct—fighting the panic. After a few seconds of standing motionless in the unfamiliar room, he remembered.

The fire, Ryan's funeral, his resignation—it all came back to him in a horrific flash. He'd taken up temporary residence in the garage apartment of his parents' lakeside house. He'd been here two weeks now. "Recovering from the trauma," they said. Hiding out was more like it.

Clint fumbled around until he found the light switch and flipped it on. Shuffling over to the small refrigerator, he retrieved a bottle of water and chugged it down, then plopped onto the sofa. He hadn't eaten supper, and water wasn't going to add any calories to his already depleted nutrition.

These days, he ate little and slept even less. His mom and dad were worried sick, he knew, but they didn't pry. They didn't ask him what he was going to do with his life since his childhood dream had literally gone up in smoke, but the question hovered in the air like a deadly gas.

On long nights like this one, Clint thought not knowing would consume his very soul. For a minute, he stared at the TV remote control on the weathered coffee table in front of him. Maybe he could lose himself in some all-night oldies or at least fall back asleep to the mindless drone of some silly show. But he didn't reach for the small gray device.

Instead, he thought about Jennifer Dawson. They'd been fairly serious until the day, three years ago, when she'd calmly explained that she couldn't take the danger of his job. *If only she'd waited*, he thought. But she hadn't. Last he'd heard, she'd married and had a kid.

Funny, though, he couldn't even remember what she looked like. Or anything they'd ever talked about, except for the last conversation when she'd asked him to give up fire-fighting. He'd known then he didn't really love her, because it never even crossed his mind to agree.

Memories like those only reminded him of how much he was going to miss his job. He had to get out. He'd known it from the minute he remembered where he was. The vastness of the starry sky and the caress of the crisp autumn breeze against his skin had become his nightly therapy.

He plunked his empty water bottle down on the table and stood. Without hesitation, he threw on a T-shirt to go with the jogging pants he slept in and grabbed his tennis shoes. The need to be outside was almost as frantic as his need to get out of bed had been a few minutes before. He pushed open the door and hurried down the wooden steps, slipping into his shoes as he went.

two

"Who's burning the bacon?" Jessa rolled over and squinted at the bedside clock. Three o'clock in the morning. "Too early for breakfast," she mumbled. She surrendered to the tiny lead weights that seemed to be attached to her eyelids, but she lingered for a second in that strange place between sleep and wakefulness. Something wasn't right.

For starters, she lived alone in the lakeside cabin she'd rented a few weeks ago. So who would be cooking breakfast? Eyes still closed, she sniffed again. Even burned bacon didn't smell that bad.

She sat up with a groan. She'd gotten a wonderful deal on the cabin rental because it was so old no one else wanted it.

Please tell me some of the ancient wiring hasn't shorted out. An electrician's bill is the last thing I need.

Still half asleep, she slid her feet into her slippers and padded down the short hall, then skidded to a stop. Smoke streamed from under the door of the water heater closet. The acrid smell burned her nostrils and her lungs. Suddenly, the sleepy haze fled from her mind as the seriousness of the situation dawned on her.

She grabbed the phone and sank to the floor, immensely thankful for the relative clarity of the lower air. Her hands shook as she dialed 911.

"911. May I help you?" The female voice was no-nonsense.

"There's a fire." She coughed.

"Ma'am, are you at 239 Lakeshore Drive?"

"Yes."

"Okay. I've already dispatched the trucks. What's your name?"

"Jessa Sykes." She looked up at the ever-thickening cloud of smoke above her head. "Please tell them to hurry."

"Jessa, listen to me. Are you alone in the house?"

"Yes." She coughed again.

"Can you see the front door?" The voice was calm but insistent.

"Yes." Thankfully, the short distance between her and the door wasn't as smoky as the area toward the kitchen.

"Go out the front door now and wait at the edge of the yard for the fire truck."

"Okay."

"I'm going to hang up now, so you can go on outside. Don't stop for anything, you hear?"

"Yes."

Jessa hung up the phone and crawled toward the door. When she was almost there, she spotted her purse at eye level on a foyer table. She grabbed it in one hand and the doorknob in the other.

Suddenly, in the eerie quietness of the hazy cabin, she heard a whimper. She gasped and yanked her hand from the doorknob as if it were scalding hot. How could she have forgotten about the puppy?

Half-starved and filthy, the little yellow pup had been sniffing around outside the flower shop yesterday. Jessa hadn't hesitated to take him home with her. She'd given him a bath, a meal, and a soft bed in the kitchen.

The kitchen. Right next to the closet that held the water heater. The kitchen that was surely filled with deadly smoke by now.

Still on her knees, she reached for the doorknob again, then stopped. If she waited for the firemen, it would probably be too late for the puppy.

She tossed her purse against the door. Then, breathing a prayer, she turned and quickly crawled back toward the whimpering sound. As she neared the kitchen, the air became blacker. She pulled the neck of her T-shirt up over her nose.

The nightlight over the stove combined with the smoke to give the room a haunted house look. She would grab the puppy from its blanket. They'd both be out in fresh air in just a minute.

Her horrified gaze fell on the empty blanket.

A feeble cry beside her sent a shiver down her spine. She turned sharply on her knees and peered behind the solid oak china cabinet. The frightened eyes of the puppy glowed in the eerie light. He appeared to be wedged just out of reach. Afraid to stand, she knelt in front of the wooden cabinet and pulled with all of her might. It didn't budge.

With a deep groan of frustration, she stretched out, face down on the floor, and reached toward the pup. The sharp corner cut into her soft flesh, but her fingertips barely brushed the soft fur. She ignored the tears that coursed down her cheeks and rested her head on her still extended arm.

Her lungs burned, but she didn't know if it was from the exertion or the smoke. Either way she had to rest for a second. *God, help me*, she prayed, as the puppy's whimpers faded from her consciousness, and she descended into a cottony haze of sleep.

❧

The lakeside drive made a circle around the placid water, and everything from ramshackle cabins to elegant mansions dotted the shore. A gentle breeze rustled the tree leaves. As he jogged quietly along the pavement, closing his eyes against the cool wind, Clint allowed peace to wash over him. He automatically put one foot in front of the other.

As his body relaxed, he stumbled on a loose pebble. He opened his eyes and grinned. He'd been asleep on his feet before, working a double shift, but he'd never fallen asleep jogging.

Sleepless nights were for the birds, like the owl that hooted softly in the big oak tree next to him. He glanced at the numbers on his lighted watch. Barely past three in the morning. Weird time for a workout.

Stress had apparently wreaked havoc on his internal chronometer. He had no idea why that would come as a surprise. It was certainly ravaging the rest of his life.

Even his senses—the same ones he used to depend on to keep him alive—were starting to play tricks on him. For a brief moment, he wondered if he was having a nervous breakdown. In the wee hours of the autumn morning, with the water lapping rhythmically on the shore a few feet away and all of the inhabitants of this sleepy little village nestled snug in their beds, Clint, the quintessential fireman, smelled smoke.

Almost of their own volition, his feet picked up speed, following the imaginary smell. He came around the bend and ground to a halt.

Clint recognized the tiny cabin as one that had been vacant for years. Tendrils of smoke were curling up from it. Small flashes of yellow and orange licked at the edges of its cedar-shingled roof like a multitude of tiny tongues.

So much for peace. He must attract fire somehow, like some men attracted women or wealth. At least it wasn't an occupied residence.

He had no doubt old Mrs. Benton would be sorry to lose the cabin that had been in her family for decades, but certainly no one else in the community would consider it a sad event.

He hurried toward the cabin, looking for a nearby water hose. There were no near neighbors, but with the brisk wind, one could never be sure what might happen.

As he came closer, all the blood in his body seemed to gel, and his heart felt like it stopped for a beat. Terror washed over him.

A small blue car was parked in the always-empty driveway.

Instincts kicking in, Clint took off at a run. When he reached the front door, he stopped, paralyzed by the gut-wrenching fear that had been his constant companion since Ryan's death.

Lord, please don't let there be anyone in there. Please don't make me do this. I can't.

He could hear the fire truck in the distance. Someone had already called them. He looked around the yard. The resident had most likely awakened, phoned 911, and was waiting on the perimeter of the property for the fire department to arrive.

He stood on the porch for a split second, frozen by indecision. Even his prayer had become more of a groaning that he couldn't put into words. Just as he tried again to step closer to the door, it slowly opened.

Clint stared as a figure collapsed on the threshold. Black smoke poured out the door with her, almost obscuring her from his view.

As if invisible restraints had been cut, Clint sprang forward and grabbed the woman, who appeared barely conscious. She clasped a lethargic puppy and a small black purse to her chest.

"Is anyone else inside?"

"No." She leaned against him as if the one word had cost her dearly.

Coughing, Clint scooped her up in his arms, puppy, purse, and all, and carried her away from the cabin, out to the edge of the lawn. He laid her carefully on the cool grass and automatically began to assess the situation. Just as he found her steady pulse, a fire truck spun into the driveway, and an ambulance was right behind it.

The woman's eyelids fluttered open. Clint was struck by the startling green color. She looked so familiar. Before he could figure out where he'd seen her before, she began to cough.

He kept his hand on her shoulder until the wracking spasms stopped. She motioned him to lean toward her.

"Puppy was stuck. . .I couldn't get him out."

"The puppy's fine, ma'am. He's right here beside you." Clint resisted the urge to smooth back the curly tendrils of red hair that framed her pale face.

She twisted her head toward the burning cabin, then moaned and coughed again. Tears tracked down her soot-blackened face. "Oh, no."

"I know it hurts to cough. Try to relax."

"No, it's my family."

"Your family?" She'd told him no one else was inside. Could she have been confused? He felt the familiar adrenaline rush. "Is someone else in the building?"

"No." Her voice was weak but sure. "My family will think it's my fault."

Clint looked back at the cabin. "I doubt that. After decades of use, wiring gets worn and old." Instinctively, he took her hand in comfort.

She squeezed it. "You saved me," she murmured. "You're a real-life hero."

The relief he'd felt when the front door opened disappeared, and a lead ball of self-disgust settled in his stomach.

Hero? Not hardly.

Before he could speak, two uniformed EMTs arrived by her side and took control of the situation. Clint stood and looked toward the cabin now engulfed in flames. Firefighters worked valiantly to contain the blaze, but from their procedures, he recognized they'd given up the structure itself as a total loss.

He'd go tell the fire chief what had happened, then get on home. He'd done all he could here. Which was not much, actually.

"Wait!"

He glanced back. The red-haired beauty, now on a stretcher between the two EMTs, motioned toward him.

He walked over to her, desperately hoping she wouldn't call him a "hero" again.

"Thank you."

Heat crept up his neck, but he nodded. Right now wasn't the place or the time to try to set the record straight.

"I know you've done enough, but will you take the puppy? At least until I figure out what I'm going to do?" Her eyes were pleading.

He nodded and scooped up the wiggling yellow puppy who seemed to have recovered completely. To his surprise, it growled and nipped at his hand.

"It's a stray," she said. "Thank you for taking him. I'm sorry I didn't have any flowers for your mother." She barely got the words out before another coughing spell started and the attendants hurried her off to the ambulance.

He wondered for a moment if she was delirious, but as the vehicle doors shut behind her, he realized why the green eyes had looked so familiar. She was the florist he'd met his first day back in town. Even in his sorry mental state, he'd been fascinated by The Flower Basket's new owner.

He turned toward the burning cabin. *Was it a twist of fate or an act of God that had thrown them together tonight?*

three

Jessa plucked at the sheet on the ER bed and shivered. A large framed print provided the only relief against the stark whiteness of the windowless room. She stared at the sun-drenched ocean scene and willed herself to soak in the warmth of the hot sand. Leaning back against the wall, she stared at the deserted beach.

The sterile room receded, and suddenly she was nine years old again, with waves washing over her head. She swam frantically for the shore, but the current pulled her under the briny water again and again.

The flood of despair washing over her now felt no less deadly. Her father had saved her that day at the beach, and she had no doubt he'd love to save her now. But at what cost?

She loved her family, but she'd moved from Georgia to get away from their watchful eyes. Instead of the smooth sailing she'd hoped for on Lake Freedom, she feared her boat had just sunk.

If only she hadn't procrastinated about buying renter's insurance. Somewhere in the charred remains of the cabin were quotes from three companies in town. She'd looked through them before going to bed and had settled on the most reasonable one, intending to take care of it first thing this morning.

Now all of her worldly possessions were gone. Well not quite all. The things she'd stored in the outdoor storage building should be fine. At the time, she'd hated putting anything in the musty old shed on the back of the property. Now she realized her reluctant decision had inadvertently saved the few items she had left to her name.

Just like her hero's decision to go on a late night excursion—jog, most likely, if his clothes were any indication—had saved her life. Why had he been so averse to being called a hero? His warm blue eyes had turned frosty when she'd used the word.

She sagged back against the wall and pulled a blanket over her legs. Even though she'd worn flannel pajama bottoms out of the burning cabin, her teeth chattered. How many times had she sat in an emergency room just like this one? Too many.

The doctor had examined her shortly after she'd been brought in, then hurried out. A lab technician had come and drawn enough blood to run every test known to mankind. What seemed like hours later, a nurse had bustled in, checked Jessa's vital signs, and heralded the doctor's second coming, but so far, he hadn't appeared. Jessa wondered what she would do when he signed her release papers.

From the corner of her eye, she caught movement as the door slowly opened. The tap that followed was obviously an afterthought on the doctor's part. The short, balding man in a white lab coat who had examined her earlier walked into the room, engrossed in an open file. He looked up from the folder. "Hi, Jessa. You feeling better?" Without waiting for a response, he began a cursory exam.

After she had taken numerous deep breaths and coughed on command several times, he nodded. "You have a little smoke inhalation. All your blood tests came back normal, though." He patted her shoulder. "I think you'll be fine with some rest." His eyes softened. "I understand you lost your home in the fire. Do I need to keep you overnight to be sure you get rest?"

"No. I'd rather go—" Her voice broke off. Go where? Where did you go when your house burned to the ground in the middle of the night? "Go to my shop."

It was not technically true. Her shop was the last place she wanted to go. There was no bed nor couch. But it would be quiet, and it would be hers.

The doctor nodded, but his eyes shone with sympathy. "Do you have a ride?"

"No. Yes." She grimaced at the hoarseness of her voice. It was bad enough to be helpless without sounding like it, too. "The fireman said my car was fine. I can walk and get it."

"Isn't that out on the lake? I don't—"

A voice on the intercom interrupted him. "Dr. Satterfield to CICU, stat. Code Blue, repeat, Code Blue."

He pinched the bridge of his nose and signed her papers. "Go ahead and check out if you want to, but wait in the reception area until I finish with this, and we'll find you a ride out to your car." He shoved the folder at her and hurried out of the room.

Jessa sat stock-still and tried to think. What choice did she have but to wait for the doctor? She didn't want to worry Evelyn and Ruby, and who else could she call in the middle of the night? Her gaze fastened on the clock. It wasn't the middle of the night anymore. In this room without windows, it was hard to believe it was morning. A few minutes past eight. Her shop would open in two hours.

If she could get a ride to her car, she could beat Doris there, get cleaned up, and rest for a while. She kept a sleeping bag and a pillow in the trunk of the car. She would throw those down on the floor and trust that her assistant would understand when she found Jessa sacked out in the back room. Tears burned her already irritated eyes.

She blinked against the hated weakness and tossed the blanket to one side, then scooted off the bed. She'd slipped into her shoes and started for the door just as another tap came. "Yes?"

A man poked his head in. "You decent?"

"Well, if I wasn't, it would be a little late."

She recognized her reluctant hero as he stepped into the room, holding the silliest looking stuffed puppy she'd ever seen.

Pushing her gloominess aside, she smiled. "That's not the pup I left you with."

He snapped his fingers and grinned. "I was hoping you wouldn't notice." His eyes, so somber in repose, twinkled like a Christmas tree when he smiled. "I knew they wouldn't let me bring the real thing, so I left him at home chewing on my best boots. I picked this little guy up at the gift shop instead." He held the toy out to her.

She took the plush puppy and squeezed it to her cheek. "It's so soft. Thank you." She marveled at the comfort that hugging an inanimate object gave her.

Suddenly she remembered the feel of this man's strong arms around her, lifting her effortlessly out of harm's way. Maybe she'd been alone too long, trying to establish her independence. She raised an eyebrow and considered her mysterious rescuer. What was it about this man that had her thinking about her single status?

He returned her gaze, refusing to look away. The silence stretched across the room like a taut rubber band.

Jessa's stomach squirmed as if one were aimed at her.

He finally spoke. "I'm Clint McFadden."

"And I'm the damsel in distress. Jessa Sykes."

He nodded. "I know."

"Oh, yeah, I guess the fireman told you."

"No, actually, my mom did."

Jessa looked at him. "McFadden?" The name sounded so familiar. "Oh, you're Jeb and Elaine's son!" She could see the resemblance now between her hero and the couple who'd been so friendly to her at church the last few weeks. "Your parents are so sweet! I just love them."

Clint ducked his head. She watched in fascination as red slowly suffused his face. How long had it been since she'd met a man who blushed? "That's good. Because my mom has given me an order. Since you like her, it'll be easier to deal with."

"An order?" Jessa couldn't imagine that either Clint or his mom thought she was in any shape to talk about flowers. Didn't they realize she was homeless, not to mention exhausted?

"When I told her about your cabin, and that I was coming to the hospital this morning to check on you, she insisted I bring you to their house as soon as the doctor released you."

"To their house?" It occurred to Jessa that she was repeating everything he said, but she couldn't help it. "Why?"

"They were hoping you'd stay with them while you figure things out."

"Oh." She absently stroked the stuffed animal while her tired mind fumbled for a tactful way to decline. Changing one pair of controlling parents for another pair wasn't her idea of becoming an independent woman. Even if this set did have an absolutely gorgeous son who blushed at the drop of a hat. "Please tell them thanks, but I've got things under control."

He raised an eyebrow and opened his mouth then shut it. "I see."

For a minute, she wondered if he really did see. He seemed to take her "No, thanks" personally. Maybe asking him for a ride to her car would take the sting out of her refusal. Surely throwing herself briefly on the mercy of her rescuer would be more palatable than waiting for the doctor to make travel arrangements for her. "Would you mind taking me to my car, though?"

"Okay. After you get your car, are you up to checking yourself into a hotel? I could follow you back into town and help you get settled." He looked at her clothes. "I know you can't wait to get into something clean."

She cringed. She knew she looked a mess, but he didn't have to spell it out so plainly with his pitying expression. "I can clean up at the shop." She glanced down at her T-shirt and pajama bottoms. They were filthy and torn. "I keep an extra set of clothes in the cabinet." Without warning, hot tears filled her eyes again. Her only set of clothes now.

"Why not wait until you get to the hotel to clean up?"

Her hero might be reluctant, but he was certainly persistent. "Actually, I think I'll just stay at the shop for a few days until I get things sorted out. There's a back room."

"At The Flower Basket?" He started to say more, then closed his mouth instead and shook his head.

She felt her defenses rise. How could she tell him that, with no insurance, every spare penny would have to be used to replace her clothes and other necessities? A hotel room was a luxury she simply couldn't afford. And allowing others to care for her came with a price tag of a different kind. But one she wasn't willing to pay, just the same. "I'd prefer to be at my own place."

"I've seen that back room," he mumbled.

She shot him a warning look, and apparently taking the hint, he changed the subject. "You ready? When I walked by the nurses' station, I overheard the doctor say you were going to be fine and that he'd released you."

"Yeah." Fine was relative, but when she stopped and thought about it, having no clothes was fairly trivial considering how things could have turned out. Shame flooded her at her ungrateful attitude a few minutes before. "I'm thankful you were in the mood for a middle-of-the-night jog."

Her heart hammered against her chest at the memory of the smoke-filled cabin, even as she grabbed her purse and clutched the stuffed puppy under her arm. She looked up at Clint. "I don't think I could have made it breathing that smoke much longer."

He nodded shortly. "Let's go."

He pushed the door open and placed his hand against the small of her back as he ushered her out. For a split second she relaxed against his palm, drawing strength from his steady presence. Then she pulled away and hurried down the vinyl-tiled hallway toward the checkout window, clutching the plush toy to her chest and barely glancing at the tall man beside her.

❧

Clint glanced over at his passenger and sighed. Every time he offered assistance of any kind, she bristled. Just like the pup she'd sent home with him last night. Food was about the only thing the skittish dog would take from him.

A fast-food restaurant on the corner caught his eye. He looked at Jessa again. It was worth a try. "You hungry? Could you eat a biscuit if I drive through here?"

She nodded, then looked down at her lap, where she still clutched her small purse and the stuffed puppy he'd brought her. "I don't think I have any cash in my purse, but I'll pay you back."

He pulled into the drive-thru lane and didn't answer. If he disagreed, she'd probably refuse to eat. If he agreed to take money from someone who'd just lost everything in a fire, he'd lose his own appetite.

"Sausage biscuit okay?"

"Mmm-hmm." While he had been looking at the menu board, she'd pulled the plush toy up and was using it for a pillow against the window.

"I'll take that as a yes," he said under his breath.

Clint ordered the food and didn't speak again until the young man at the second window handed him the white sack. "Thanks," he said softly.

Light snoring drifted from somewhere beneath the red curls that had fallen across Jessa's face. After what she'd gone through, she had to be wiped out. How tempting it was to take care of her. But she didn't want him to. He snorted softly. Who was he kidding? Taking care of people obviously wasn't his strong suit. The best thing he could do was stay as far away as possible from the sleeping beauty in his passenger seat.

He drove slowly down the lakeshore drive and resisted the urge to circle a few times so she could get some rest. All that was left of the cabin were some ashes and lingering smoke. He wished he could have spared her the painful experience of seeing her former home. Reluctantly, he pulled his Jeep into the spot beside her car. When he turned the key off, she jerked awake.

"Oh! We're here. I'm sorry." She ran her hand over her face, then through her unruly curls in a move Clint found endearing. When she looked out the windshield at the smoking heap, her green eyes widened, then filled with tears. She bit her lip and turned toward her window.

Clint sat in silence for a few seconds, watching her shoulders shake. Finally, he'd had all he could stand. "Jessa?"

She shook her head but didn't turn back toward him.

"It's natural for you to be devastated. A fire is like any other trauma. . .robbery or even a violent crime." A memory of Ryan saying those same words to the men at the station flashed through Clint's mind. His friend had never doubted, never underestimated the danger of a fire. Clint put his hand on her shoulder.

She stiffened, and he prepared himself for her to tell him to mind his own business. Instead, she swung around and collapsed in his arms. Her heart-wrenching sobs touched a place deep in his heart where he'd locked away his grief over Ryan's death. Tears edged his eyes, and as he held her, he acknowledged the pain of his own loss as well.

"Do you want to talk about it?" he asked softly.

For a minute, she didn't speak, clinging to him as he breathed in the smoke smell from her strawberry-blond curls. Then she drew back and swiped at the tears with the back of her hand. She nodded.

As Jessa told her story, Clint's mouth grew dry. She'd risked her life for a stray pup. Had he been jogging down Lakeshore Drive at that minute? Or had he already noticed the smoke?

"I bathed him and made him a bed in the kitchen, but then when the fire started, I guess he wedged himself behind the china cabinet. And I couldn't get him out. . ." Her voice rose in panic.

Without warning, she shivered and buried her head in his shoulder again, as if terrified of the scene unfolding before her mind's eye.

He held her quietly for a few minutes, stroking her hair, until she calmed. His own heart clenched as he imagined her trying to get to the puppy.

"I stretched out on the floor. Smoke was everywhere. I could barely touch him. At first he licked my hand." Her words were spoken against Clint's shirt. She sat up straight again, and he released her but held on to her hand.

"Then I got so tired, I had to lay my head down and rest."

"You relaxed in the smoke?" How could that be? When that happened, it was over. Unless a rescuer got there in time. And he hadn't. Bile rose in his throat. He'd been paralyzed with fear on the lawn.

"Yes, I remember praying, but then my head was just so heavy, so I rested it on my arm. The next thing I felt was sharp pain at my wrist over and over again." Her voice held a note of wonderment.

"Pain from what?" Usually even if victims were rescued after they passed out, they had no memory of pain.

Jessa's attempt at a chuckle came out as a half-sob. "The puppy was biting me." She unclasped her hand from his and turned her arm over. Several red, angry welts on her wrist attested to her tale.

"And that woke you?"

"Yes, and I tried one more time to grab the pup. I could barely pinch his skin, but it was enough to unwedge it. When I got him in my arms, I crawled to the front door. But after I opened it, I couldn't go any further."

"And that's where I came in." The tightness in his chest eased a notch. He'd been afraid that in her post-fire shock, she'd imagined him coming into the house and rescuing her. But she'd been more right than he'd first known. Using Clint, God had saved her from the fire.

Jessa relaxed into his embrace again. "Yes," she whispered. "You saved the day." Her words were thick with tears.

Unexpected anger surged through him. What happened to God being no respecter of persons? Why had He allowed Clint to help save a stranger but not his best friend?

four

As she'd told Clint what happened in the cabin, Jessa's heavy heart had grown considerably lighter, but she still couldn't believe she was crying in Clint McFadden's arms. What had happened to her philosophy of standing on her own two feet? Counting on God and no one else? Along came a little trouble, and she'd tossed her newfound independence out the window.

She pulled back from his embrace and willed the sobs to subside. "I'm sorry." A shuddering sigh cut off her next words, and she gave Clint a teary grin. "My mom always called that 'snubbing,' and I couldn't ever keep from doing it after the waterworks stopped."

With his thumb, he gently wiped the tears from her cheeks. "It's kind of cute if you ask me."

She was startled by his words, and if the red that crept up his face was any indication, so was he. "Thanks. I think." She nodded toward the cabin. "Do you think we could look around?"

He shook his head. "Not yet. Not at the actual site anyway. It's not safe."

"What about the outbuilding? I think it would be okay to check out the things in there, don't you?"

"Sure."

He opened his Jeep door and jumped out. She unbuckled and located her keys in her purse, but before she could touch the handle, he was at her side, holding the door for her.

They walked together across the green lawn. She tried to ignore the smoking heap that had been her home, keeping her eyes instead on the old red storage shed that housed what was left of her belongings. She kicked a dead limb and stared out at the lake. "I've been looking forward to autumn here. The crispness of the air, the gorgeous fall colors, the smell of burning leaves. . ." She sniffed the still acrid air. "Right now I'd just as soon never smell anything burning again."

"I feel the same way." Clint's voice was quiet.

Jessa cast a sideways glance at him. Something about this whole thing had definitely touched a nerve with him. His solemn expression went beyond sympathy for a neighbor who'd had a fire. She remembered that day she'd seen him in the flower shop. Even then he'd seemed mysterious. What was his story?

Whatever it was, he was every bit the gentleman. As they approached the padlocked door, he motioned to her for the key, and she handed it over. He opened the lock, then stood back for her to go in first.

Even in the dank, musty surroundings, Jessa felt like a kid in a toy store. She'd forgotten how many things she'd stored here due to the compact nature of the cabin. For a few minutes, she just soaked in the joy of ownership while Clint looked on with a smile.

Her bicycle was propped against the paneling. She touched its cool surface, then quickly moved on to her next find. Plastic boxes of pictures, neatly labeled, were stacked along one wall. She remembered how she'd struggled with putting them out here, but now she was so glad she had. She slipped the top off one and pulled out a handful.

She'd almost forgotten Clint's presence until he spoke. "May I?" He indicated the pictures she had in her hand.

She glanced down at them. Her random sampling had produced mostly photos of her youth. An odd thing to share with a relative stranger. But for some reason, she didn't think of Clint that way anymore. The embrace in the car, combined with the fact that he saved her life, had broken the ice.

"Sure." She handed them to him and grabbed another bunch from the box.

They looked through the photos in silence for a few minutes. Then Clint frowned. She instinctively looked to see what picture had elicited the response. It was a picture of her with her parents and sister. They were standing in front of a brick wall that Jessa knew all too well. The only part of the building's name that could be seen was G-E-N-E-R. The memory was not a happy one for Jessa, but why would Clint frown?

Before she could ask, he held the picture out to her. "Were you in the hospital when you were small?"

"What makes you think that's a hospital?"

"Well, I figured the letters probably spelled 'General,' which is often in the name of a hospital."

Jessa glared at him, inexplicably irritated by his reasoning. "It could be the General Foods headquarters."

"Yeah, except for the plastic bracelet on the adorable little redhead's arm."

"Yes, I was in the hospital." Jessa stuffed the rest of the pictures back in the box, suddenly disenchanted with her walk down memory lane.

Clint deposited the batch he held into the plastic container as well and carefully closed the lid. At least he appeared to be perceptive enough to let it drop.

Jessa turned to the opposite side of the shed. "My kayak!" She grinned at the boat she'd suspended from the ceiling with a simple pulley system in one corner. "You old sweetie."

She reached up and patted the fiberglass hull.

Clint ran his hand over the sharp grooves on the bottom. "From the looks of those grooves on the bottom, it's done some whitewater rafting. Do you take it out on the river?"

"Every time I get the chance."

"By yourself?" His worried voice irritated her. She understood why her family thought she was so fragile, but why would a stranger?

"Sometimes. It converts into a two-person craft, so occasionally I have a friend go with me." She grimaced. "Or I did in Georgia anyway." She stopped polishing an imaginary smudge with the tail of her T-shirt and looked back at the tall man in the doorway. "Do you ride the rapids?"

He shook his head. "I did when I was younger but not anymore. Doesn't that seem a little risky to you?"

Uh-oh, here it comes. "That's too dangerous for you, Jessa." No matter where she went, she couldn't seem to escape it.

"I've taken enough of your time." She wiped the dust off her hands onto her flannel pants and stepped out of the building. She waited for him to exit, then pulled the door shut and secured the padlock. "Well, thank you for bringing me out here."

At her abrupt words, he frowned. "Can I follow you into town? I know you can't be feeling all that great."

"No, thanks. I'll be okay."

She started walking back toward the vehicles, hoping he'd take the hint.

They retraced their steps across the yard in awkward silence.

At her car door, she stuck out her hand in a purposely businesslike manner. "Thank you again for all you've done."

He looked at her proffered hand for a few seconds, then shook it firmly.

She slid into her car seat, closing the door behind her. He held her gaze through the window, then slowly turned toward the Jeep.

Amazing how badly she'd wanted him to continue holding her in those strong arms. How could she be interested in someone who would obviously protect her at all costs? Getting involved with a man like that would be the death knell to her fight for independence. In her mind, she paraphrased the warning she'd always felt coming from her family. Only this time it was true.

He's too dangerous for you, Jessa.

Clint stared through the car window at the woman who had fallen into his shattered heart last night when he'd carried her to safety. For the first time since Ryan's death, he knew something besides rage and sorrow.

Her freckles stood out against her alabaster skin, and her green eyes looked huge. She'd be okay? He thought that was definitely debatable, but he didn't want to start an argument.

He opened the Jeep door and saw the stuffed puppy and her purse lying in the passenger seat. He grabbed them, along with one of the biscuits from the sack.

She was adjusting something on the dash but looked up when he tapped on the window. The glass rolled smoothly down, and she reached for her purse and the toy. "Thanks."

"No problem. Here's your biscuit, as well."

"Oh."

He could see from her expression that she didn't quite remember the stop at the fast-food place. It was a wonder she hadn't forgotten her own name with all she'd been through.

"I have some cash at the shop. . ."

He pushed the biscuit into her hand. "We'll deal with that

later. You go get cleaned up and get some rest."

She nodded, weariness filling her eyes.

He waited until she was on the road, then drove the short distance to his parents' house. He called his mom from the cell phone to tell her Jessa wasn't coming. He just wasn't up to going to the main house right now.

When he opened the door to his garage apartment, Jessa's puppy barked a greeting and ran toward him. Clint reached down to give him a pat, but the skittish animal darted behind the couch. Like owner, like pet, he thought wryly.

He would have to rig up some kind of leash in order to take the dog outside. There was no way he could be trusted to return, once loose.

"I'd better do that right now," Clint muttered to the shivering lump of fur behind the couch. Then he headed to the closet. "Before you make a mess and I have to clean it up."

A knock on the door brought him back into the living room empty-handed. "Hold on, Sport. I promise I'll find something."

His mother stood on the doorstep with a leash and collar in her hand. "This was Sparky's. I thought you might need it."

He gave her a hug and a kiss on the cheek. "Thanks, Mom. You always could read my mind."

She frowned, worry lines creasing her normally smooth forehead. Without waiting to be asked, she sank to the couch, so he followed suit.

"Well, I can't anymore. For example, I have no idea what you'll think about the decision your dad and I made this morning."

"What decision?"

"We're going to stay at the lake house until Christmas instead of going back to the ranch right away."

"Because of me." He knew the words sounded flat, but he couldn't help it. The last thing he wanted was to throw a cog in his parents' life.

His mom reached over and took his hand. "Not just because of you. You know we love to do things out of the ordinary once in a while. It keeps life exciting."

"And?" The word had been unspoken, but Clint could feel it.

"And because of Jessa." She grimaced. "What an awful situation she's in."

"I told you she refused to come here." Clint wondered if his mom had misunderstood their cell phone conversation earlier. "How can you help her?"

"Your dad and I are willing, and she needs help. God will work out the how."

A rush of bitterness flooded Clint's heart. Like He worked things out for Ryan when He put Clint within yelling distance but not close enough to reach Ryan through the fire? Clint's belief in God had never wavered, but these days he found himself questioning His willingness to look after His own. "Sometimes, even God can't help. Or won't."

His mom squeezed his hand, pulling him back to the present. "Do you remember when you were little and used to tell me all the time that you wanted to 'take care of fires' when you grew up?"

Clint nodded. He had wanted to be a fireman for as long as he could remember.

"One day when you said that, I couldn't resist. I looked into your solemn little face and said, 'Who will take care of you in the fire, Clint?' And I'll never forget what you said. Do you remember?"

Clint shook his head.

"You said, 'Don't be silly, Mama. Same as always. God will.' "

She brushed away a tear and hugged him. Then she stood. "Even though you're grown now, it's still true, Clint. Same as always. God will."

After the door closed behind her, Clint didn't move. Had every remnant of that courageous little boy with the adult-sized faith died in the fire with Ryan?

five

Jessa parked behind the shop and rested her forehead on the steering wheel. She'd made it with thirty minutes to spare. No time for a nap, but she could get cleaned up a little before Doris arrived. Close on the assistant's heels would be walk-in customers. The monthlong Grand Opening celebration continued to bring in a lively crowd. Jessa was thankful for the success, but today she'd be happy with some peace and quiet.

When she unlocked the back door and stepped into her shop, a surge of determination rushed through her. The cottage she'd rented was gone, as were most of her possessions, but this shop—her dream—was still here. Even after last night's loss, somehow, with God's help, she would make a go of this. The independence that came with running her own flower shop was a dream worthy of sacrifice.

But if she didn't clean herself up, she'd scare the customers away and kill her own dream. One glance in the bathroom mirror pulled a gasp from her lungs. Her hair was a tangled mess, and her face and clothes were covered in soot. She washed up as best she could and changed clothes but decided her hair would have to wait until after the shop closed. She tucked it up under a bright yellow cap with a smiley face on the front of it. *Nothing like putting on a happy face—literally.* Just as she finished dressing, she heard Doris's key in the door.

She hated to jump straight in with the news of her cabin burning, so she settled for "Hi."

"Jessa! Are you okay?" Doris's face was tight with concern.

"I'm fine. I just look—" Her words were cut off as Doris crossed the room and enfolded her in a hug.

"I've been praying ever since Paul got the call."

"Your husband?"

"Yes. He's a volunteer fireman. We heard the news over his radio at three o'clock." The normally composed woman looked as though she might burst into tears any second.

"Doris, thank you so much. I really am fine, but I look—"

"You look exhausted. I didn't know how to reach you. So I just came on in and hoped I'd hear from you."

Jessa grinned. Doris had said more in the past minute than she had in the two weeks she'd been working with her. "Well, here I am. If you think you can handle things, though, I'm going to fix me a pallet in the back room and lie down for a while. I'll be up by the afternoon rush." She glanced at her feet and wiggled her toes. "I won't have any shoes though, unless you count the slippers I wore out of the fire, so I'll have to stay behind the counter."

"Oh, dear. Don't give this old shop another thought. I know how to run it just fine." She guided Jessa into the back. "Holler if you need me." She shut the door.

Jessa stared at the closed door and chuckled. Why did she feel rejected? She knew Doris was trying to be helpful, but Jessa's adrenaline was pumping at the abrupt dismissal. She stomped out to the car and retrieved the pillow and sleeping bag from the trunk. When she got her pallet made, she tossed and turned for an hour before finally dozing off to sleep.

☙

"Jessa?"

She rubbed her eyes and looked up at Doris. "Is it lunchtime already?"

"Actually, it's closing time. I just locked the door." Doris nodded toward the tiny table and chair in the corner. "I asked Seth to pick up a sandwich and some chips for you. Speaking of Seth, he has one more delivery to do when he gets back from this one. Since you were going to be here to let him in, I thought I'd go on home."

Jessa sat up. "Great. Thanks, Doris."

"No problem. Have you decided what you're going to do?"

"Not yet. I'm probably going to stay here for a few days."

"In the shop?" Her incredulous words so closely echoed Clint's that Jessa felt her defenses rising.

"Yes, for a few days," she repeated. "Until I figure out what I'm going to do."

"You know. . ." Doris's voice softened. "Amy's in college, and Paul and I have that empty bedroom."

"I appreciate it, Doris. I really do. I'm going to stay here, but thanks for such a generous offer."

"If you change your mind, just let me know."

"Okay."

She breathed a sigh of relief as Doris left. Her motherly attitude was sweet, but sometimes it drove Jessa crazy. She'd been smothered with concern enough to last a lifetime.

She clamored to her feet and stretched her arms to the ceiling. "Oomph." A sore place in her back grabbed her. She rolled her shoulders to relax her tense muscles. Could she feel any worse if she'd been run over by a truck? But what had she expected when she made her bed on the thinly carpeted concrete floor? Sweet dreams?

Remembering the McFaddens' kind invitation, as well as Doris's, Jessa grimaced. Independence was wonderful, but it wasn't very cushiony.

A knock sounded at the back door, and Jessa hobbled over to answer. "Who is it?"

"Seth."

When the teen saw Jessa, he ran one hand over his crew cut and whistled. "You okay?"

"Yes." The cap had slipped off in her stretching, and since she was alone, she hadn't replaced it. No wonder the boy looked a little frightened. She quickly put it on.

"I'm sorry about your cabin." His eyes darkened with an emotion Jessa couldn't pinpoint. "It's tough not having somewhere to stay."

"I'm going to stay here for a few days."

"Here?" His face looked troubled.

"Yeah, but it'll be fine. So this is your last delivery today?"

"Yep. Mrs. Grantham's nephew ordered flowers for her birthday."

"She's in Garrington Manor where Evelyn and Ruby live, isn't she?"

"Yeah."

"Do you see Ruby much?" Evelyn had mentioned that the boy was completely devoted to her sister, who had hired him for deliveries when he was barely old enough to pull a red wagon.

Seth's face turned red, but he nodded. "Every day."

"That's wonderful. I know she appreciates it."

His face turned an even deeper shade of red, and he mumbled something unintelligible.

Jessa had almost forgotten how sensitive teens could be. He must have been embarrassed that she realized he cared about Ruby.

She sat at the table and ate her sandwich while he went into the front and retrieved the arrangement.

"See you tomorrow," she called as he went out the door.

She thought she heard a grunt in answer, but she wasn't

even sure of that. She threw the deadbolt behind him and turned her attention toward her sandwich.

As she finished the last bite, a knock sounded on the door again. Sure Seth had forgotten something, she flipped the deadbolt and yanked it open. Someday, she'd learn not to assume she knew who was at the door. Just as he had her first day, when she'd thought Evelyn had forgotten something, Clint McFadden filled the doorway. This time, though, he grinned broadly, a bag tossed over his shoulder like Santa.

⋇

Clint chuckled at the surprised expression on Jessa's face. With the baseball cap on and freckles playing across her nose, she looked about twelve. "Expecting someone else?"

"Actually, yes. I thought my delivery boy had forgotten something."

"Disappointed?"

"No." Her face turned red. "Well, not that I would have been disappointed—oh, never mind."

Clint watched the play of emotions across her face as she struggled to answer his trick question. He'd teased her without thinking.

The phone rang and Jessa jumped, then smiled. "Saved by the bell. Just a minute."

As she disappeared into the front room to answer the phone, Clint maneuvered the bag he'd brought inside and shut the door. He shifted from one foot to the other as Jessa's voice drifted back to him.

"Yes, I'm getting settled in."

Clint leaned against the wall. If the caller was someone close to Jessa, he'd be here for a while if they didn't know about the fire yet.

"The shop is doing well. Um, yes, we just closed. Of course I sound tired. I told you about our monthlong Grand Opening celebration, didn't I? Well, today was the last day."

After a few more generic phrases, she ended the call with an "I love you, too, and tell all the family the same."

When she walked back in and saw him standing there, he could tell she'd forgotten his presence for a minute.

"Oh." An unspoken *You're still here* hung in the air. "Sorry, that was my mom."

"You didn't tell her about the fire?" He kept his tone deliberately soft so that she wouldn't think he was condemning her.

"No." Her face grew red. "I didn't see any reason to worry them."

Clint knew his family was unusual in their closeness, and even they had been known to keep secrets, but he was pretty sure if one of them lost all their belongings and almost lost their lives in a fire, he'd know about it within two or three hours of the catastrophe. Clint's mind raced back to Jessa's words after the fire—"My family will think it's my fault."

Apparently she had her own reasons for not telling her family. "My mom sent you some stuff." He handed her the large black garbage bag his mother had packed so carefully. "I'm not sure what's in there, but there are some clothes, I know. She said you were about her size."

Jessa nodded. "Thanks." She pulled her cap bill down a little farther, then motioned over her shoulder. "I'd invite you in, but there's not really a place to sit."

Clint looked at the rumpled pallet on the floor. He knew she was barely short of closing the door on him, but he was reluctant to leave her here alone in the tiny room. "Mom and Dad have a huge guest room. They would love for you to stay with them. Mom thinks you're great."

"I think she's pretty wonderful, too, but I'd better just stay here. Thanks, though." Her smile was a little forced.

"Have it your way. If you need anything, give me a call."

"I will. Thanks again. And tell your mom thanks for the clothes."

"No problem." Clint closed the door behind him and walked slowly to his Jeep. How could one tiny woman be so stubbornly independent?

six

Jessa took the last item out of the bag and laid it on the table, then sank down into the chair. Tears burned her eyes. When she'd seen the black garbage bag in Clint's hand, she'd gratefully expected a hodgepodge of old clothes and possibly even a pair of shoes. What she'd gotten instead was manna from heaven.

Five outfits suitable for wearing to work were folded neatly together on top. A green short set and a pair of comfortable-looking jeans and a button-up shirt were next, followed by two pairs of pumps and a pair of new-looking white tennis shoes. And discreetly tucked together were pajamas and four sets of undergarments. Amazingly, everything was her size.

To her delight, beneath the clothes, an overnight case revealed shampoo, conditioner, a new toothbrush, toothpaste, and a variety of makeup and toiletry items. She'd planned to deplete her petty cash and run down to the discount store before it closed at nine, but she would be able to stay at the shop and wash her hair instead. Even a hairdryer and curling iron were included.

When Jessa took out the overnight case and four bath towels and washcloths below it, a few lumps were still left in the plastic bag. Inside were three Christian fiction books she'd been eager to read. The last lump in the bag was a Bible. When Jessa opened the black leather cover, the handwritten inscription took her breath away.

To Jessa, who believes in new beginnings and has the courage to make them happen.

With love, The McFaddens

In the few conversations she'd had with Elaine at church, Jessa had apparently revealed more of herself than she realized. Although where Elaine had gotten the idea that she had courage, she couldn't imagine. It must be positive thinking on the older woman's part. Sort of an "if you think it, it will be true" idea.

Still smiling at the encouraging words, she stood and looked at her pile of treasures on the table. Now to get the place organized. A quick search revealed a small unused shelf under the counter in the main room of the shop. She dragged the wobbly frame into the back and dusted the plastic surface before stacking her new clothes on it. When she put her toiletries in the bathroom, one look at the short, small sink confirmed there was no way she could bend over and wash her hair in it.

She grabbed the shampoo, conditioner, and a towel and carried them to the big sink built into the counter. The deep sink would be perfect for shampooing her hair.

After her hair was scrubbed clean and dry, Jessa changed into the pajamas Elaine had sent and plopped down on her sleeping bag with one of the books. The shop phone rang, and she jerked aright. Who would be calling here at this hour?

She hurried into the front and snatched up the receiver. "Flower Basket."

"You don't belong there." The caller's voice rattled like gravel, but it was impossible to tell if it was a man or a woman.

"This is The Flower Basket," she repeated.

A loud click resounded in her ear, followed by the dial tone.

She stared at the receiver, her mind racing. Had it been a random call? Or had the message been for her? She shivered. She hung up the phone and with her hand still on it, murmured a prayer both for herself and the caller.

She tiptoed through the darkened front room of the shop and touched the deadbolt and lock to be sure they were thrown. Satisfied the front was secure, she checked the back door as well.

Still rattled, but feeling more secure, she forced herself to lie down with her book again. An hour later her eyes began to grow heavy, so she turned off the light and lay in the darkness. Even with the hard bed, cramped quarters, and unsettling phone call, she had a heart full of thanks to pour out to God before drifting off to sleep.

&

"Clint?"

At the sight of the stranger, the yellow pup skittered behind Clint's legs, tangling the leash around him.

"Yes." He stepped out of the twisted line and looked questioningly at the smiling man who'd sought him out midmorning in his parents' backyard.

The man stuck out his hand. "Don Morgan, Lakehaven fire chief. We spoke briefly at the cabin fire the other night. But between it being dark and me not being in uniform today, I didn't figure you'd remember me."

Clint shook his hand. "I'm sorry I didn't. What can I do for you?" He wondered for a second if the department suspected arson in the cabin fire. Jessa said they'd told her it was definitely old wiring, but why else would the fire chief come to see him?

"I wanted to thank you." He nodded across the lake in the general direction of Jessa's cabin. "You made our job a lot easier the other night."

"I just happened to be in the right place at the right time."

"And you just happened to know what to do. I understand you're a firefighter."

Clint gripped the leash handle so tightly that it cut into his hand. "Not anymore."

"We never have a shortage of boys who think being a 'fire-man' sounds glamorous and exciting. But we could use an experienced firefighter like you in the department."

"I'm sorry, but you've got the wrong man."

The fire chief nodded. "If you say so." He glanced up toward the house. "Your dad sure bragged on you while you were down there in Little Rock." He clapped his big hand on Clint's shoulder and squeezed. "We'd consider ourselves lucky to have you."

Clint kicked at the ground with the toe of his boot and met the man's all-too-understanding eyes. "I appreciate it, but I'm not interested."

"I understand. Let me know if you change your mind." To his credit, Chief Morgan appeared to be a man who knew when to stop. He disappeared as quickly as he'd come.

Clint sank to the ground and scooped up a handful of pebbles. He tossed one into the lake and watched the small circle grow.

In the great scheme of things, did God throw the rock? Or did He just control the ripples once they were in play? In spite of the bitter taste in Clint's mouth, he couldn't even consider a third possibility—that God turned his back on the rock throwing and let whatever happened happen.

Clint threw the remaining handful of pebbles in the water at once.

The pup beside him yelped.

"Sorry, buddy." Clint ruffled the hair on the dog's head and pushed to his feet. "If I've worried Dad enough for him to sic the fire chief on me, it's time for me to get a job."

He left the puppy barking anxiously in the apartment and hurried to his Jeep. The sooner he found work, the sooner his family would quit hounding him about going back into firefighting.

As he headed toward the town center, he realized that the nearest newspaper box wasn't far from The Flower Basket. He should probably stop in and see how Jessa managed sleeping on the floor last night. He shook his head at her stubbornness.

His mom hadn't seemed discouraged by Jessa's refusal to stay at their house. "Everyone has to come to terms with things in their own time," she'd said. He'd wondered if she was partly letting him know that they understood his need for time.

As he cruised slowly down the road, he glanced at the Tri-Lake Security office. In some brochures, the town of Lakehaven boasted five lakes, but only three were big enough to be recognized as official lakes. Tri-Lake Security patrolled around those three, including Lake Millicent, where Clint's parents lived. A large *Help Wanted* sign obscured most of their window. Clint slowed to a stop.

The bored blond at the desk handed him an application. "Fill it out here or take it home. 'Sup to you."

Clint sat in the vinyl chair and balanced the clipboard on the aluminum arm. He filled out the blanks quickly, signed the release for a background check, and handed it back.

She looked up as though surprised he was still there. "Oh, okay, I'll give that to John when he comes in."

Clint nodded, relieved that he'd taken one step toward the future.

Within minutes, he was pulling into the parking lot at The

Flower Basket. A middle-aged woman with a sweet smile greeted him when he entered.

"Is Jessa here?" he asked, suddenly feeling foolish. Why would she want to see him? The last time they'd talked, she hadn't been exactly friendly.

Just as the woman opened her mouth to answer, Jessa stepped through the doorway. She was wearing green, and her eyes sparkled to match it. Her ponytail bounced as she walked over to him. "Clint, I was just thinking about you," she said with a smile.

"Uh-oh. I'm afraid to ask." He could feel his ears grow hot, but he grinned.

"No, nothing bad." She chuckled. "Even though I called your mom and told her how much I appreciated the things she sent, I know I didn't really thank you like I should have. . .for all the help you gave me, both during the fire and after. I was hoping I'd get a chance to tell you that."

"No problem. As a matter of fact, here's your chance to pay me back."

"Really?" She drew her eyebrows together. "What do you mean?"

"I'm starving. I was hoping you might take pity on me."

"Sure." The twinkle was back in her eyes. "I've got some peanut butter and jelly in the back. I'll be glad to fix you a sandwich."

He resisted the urge to agree just to see her shock. "I was actually hoping you'd eat at Skinny's with me."

In her clear green eyes, he could see the emotions flicker as she considered his request. The mental tally must have ended in his favor, because she nodded. "Let me grab my purse."

"I don't suppose it would do any good to tell you I wanted lunch to be my treat."

"Nope, I don't suppose it would," she replied, looking rather smug.

"I'll settle for what I can get," he muttered under his breath as she left the room again.

seven

Jessa's hands shook as she retrieved her purse from the tiny shelf in the back room. "I was just thinking about you"? What kind of thing was that to say? She *had* been thinking about him, of course, and she'd been so surprised and happy to see him that the words had popped out.

She pressed her hands against her warm cheeks. If she wasn't more mindful of her words, he'd get the impression that she was interested in him as more than a friend. And since he had "protector" stamped all over him, that couldn't be further from the truth.

Still, a girl had to eat.

With that reassurance, she hurried out to meet her lunch partner.

As they stepped into the sunny day, Clint motioned toward the Jeep with a questioning expression on his face.

"Let's walk." Jessa tilted her face to the blue sky, admiring the clouds that wafted by like dandelion seeds blown by a wishing child. "It's gorgeous."

"Yes, gorgeous."

She looked at him sharply. He offered her a crooked grin, but she still couldn't tell if he was referring to her or simply agreeing with her assessment of the day.

They strolled in comfortable silence to the little eatery on the corner. Clint held the door and, once at the table, pulled a chair out for her. If he was trying to impress her, it was working.

The waitress brought the menus, hand lettered and fancifully colored with crayons. "The special of the day is a pecan chicken salad sandwich with fresh sliced tomatoes and a garden salad." She pulled out her pad and poised her pen as if at the starting line of the Indy 500. "What can I get you to drink?"

"Sweet tea," they chorused.

"Alrighty then." The waitress, whose name tag proclaimed her to be *Darlene*, smiled. "You all must have been together a long time."

"About ten minutes," Clint quipped and grinned.

Jessa smiled at his easy manner.

Without missing a beat, Darlene slapped Clint playfully on the shoulder. "Do y'all know what you want to eat? Or should I come back with your drinks?"

Jessa nodded. "I'll have the special."

"Make that two."

"Dressing?" The waitress arched one eyebrow.

"Ranch," they said simultaneously.

Jessa braced herself for Darlene to make some further comment, but the waitress apparently remembered belatedly that she might want a tip when the meal was over. She left without another word.

"She must have remembered her tip," Clint said with a wry grin.

Jessa put her hand to her mouth. "That's what I was thinking."

"Oh, no." Clint looked furtively around the room. He held up his napkin-wrapped silverware like a microphone and lowered his voice. "Little did the beautiful florist realize on that 'gorgeous' August day, when she wandered into Skinny's Eatery that she was entering another dimension. . .one where you couldn't have an original thought. Because Skinny's was a secret portal to. . .'The Twilight Zone.' "

Jessa burst out laughing. "You just disproved your own theory. I never would have thought of that in a million years."

"Yeah, but it still wasn't an original thought." He hummed a few bars of the theme song to *The Twilight Zone* and grinned.

"You've got a point." Jessa chuckled again. "One of my favorite authors has a saying on her books, 'Expect the Unexpected.' Maybe I should make that my motto concerning you." She hoped he couldn't hear her heart slamming against her ribs. He'd definitely called her beautiful that time.

"I've had worse said about me." Clint sat back as Darlene returned with the tall glasses of tea and placed them on the table.

"Thanks," Clint said, smiling at the waitress. "Do you have any straws?"

Darlene pulled one out of her brown apron pocket, then looked at Jessa, who blushed but nodded. "I'll take one, too, please."

"Umm-hum." The waitress handed Jessa a straw, pursed her lips, and hurried back to the kitchen.

"So how do you like camping out?"

"Well, I don't know," Jessa drawled. "The stars aren't quite as bright as they were when I was young."

"Sore back, huh?"

She grimaced and unwrapped her straw. "Killing me. If I don't get a bed soon, I'll have to find a chiropractor who offers a frequent-visitor plan."

"I know you think I'm going to remind you that there's a perfectly good bed at Mom and Dad's." Clint took a sip of his tea.

"Even if I was thinking that, I'd never admit it out loud." She brought her finger to her lip in a *shh* motion and nodded toward Darlene, who was filling coffee cups two tables over.

"Well, you'd be wrong anyway. I was just going to say that you can get an inflatable mattress or even a foam mat to go under your sleeping bag."

She nodded. "I think the blow-up kind would take up too much room. The other might work, though. Good idea."

"Even though I'm not sold on it making a good home for you, I like what you've done with The Flower Basket. With Mom's obsession with flowers, I've been in there several times over the years. It was always a nice shop, but you've given it flair."

"Thank you," Jessa murmured, but the pleasure she felt was immeasurable.

"Have you always wanted to be a florist?"

"No, not really." She chuckled. "When I was little, my burning ambition was to be a roller-skating carhop, but then as I grew older, I realized how much pleasure flowers bring to people. So, I sacrificed my dream job for a lifetime of arranging flowers."

"So, in other words, that bouncy ponytail is all that remains of your childhood dream."

"Well, yeah, that and the roller skates tucked in my—" She drew in a sharp breath, suddenly feeling as if she'd been sucker punched. She didn't even have a cedar chest anymore, much less her treasured roller skates.

Understanding shone in Clint's blue eyes, and he took her hand across the table. "There's nothing wrong with grieving some material things, Jessa."

She ducked her head as hot tears splashed down her cheeks. How could he know how guilty she felt for crying over an old pair of skates?

"People mean well when they say, 'It's just stuff,' but they've never been through a fire." The tenderness in his voice soaked into her weary heart like a soothing balm. "I know those skates held memories that weren't captured anywhere but in the cracked leather and tied together laces." He rubbed her finger softly with his thumb. "Anywhere but your heart, that is. It may be harder to remember without the tangible item, but you can do it if you try."

"Thanks." Her voice came out husky, and she cleared her throat. His words had been exactly what she'd needed to hear.

"Two pecan chicken salad sandwiches with garden salads on the side." Darlene placed their lunches on the table with a flourish and slapped the empty tray against her thigh. "Is there anything else I can get for you?"

They shared a cautious look and shook their heads.

"I was afraid to even think of asking for anything else," Jessa said after Darlene had disappeared into the kitchen. "Just in case you were about to ask for the same thing."

"Do you like tomatoes?" Clint asked suddenly.

"Love them."

"We've broken free of The Twilight Zone then. I can't stand them. As a matter of fact, you can have mine."

"Whew. I'm glad we're out of there. It was making me nervous."

"Really? I thought it was kind of fun, agreeing on everything."

"Well, it didn't make me nervous enough to take away my appetite." She cleared her throat and grinned. "I'd love to have your tomatoes."

He carefully transferred the red slices to her plate.

Jessa hesitated, but when Clint didn't make a move to say the blessing for the food, she bowed her head and silently thanked God for the delicious-looking meal. She had no idea if he prayed or not, but she noticed he didn't pick up his own fork until she looked up. They ate in silence for a few minutes.

"This is delicious," Jessa exclaimed. She looked around at the crowded tables. "No wonder this place is packed."

"Skinny is a legend around here," Clint said. "And he's famous for his desserts."

"Dessert?" Jessa asked. "How can anyone eat dessert after filling up on this mouthwatering food?"

Clint shrugged. "We'll have to drop by some Saturday afternoon and just have dessert."

"Our 'just' desserts?" Jessa quipped, but the meaning of his words sent her pulse racing. That sounded suspiciously like plans for a date.

&

When Clint got back to the apartment, the dog scratched at his leg, anxious to go out. Jessa would owe him one when she got back a completely housebroken puppy.

The thought of Jessa brought a smile to his face as he walked along the water's edge with the dog. He'd never met a woman like her. Her sense of humor and interests meshed with his so completely.

The yellow pup stretched out at the edge of the water. Clint yanked on the leash, and the puppy yelped.

"Sorry, you little rapscallion. You were about to fall in."

He was no better than the dog, he thought ruefully, fascinated by something he had no business pursuing.

Jessa needed a strong man who could protect her and take care of her, not a man who'd lost his faith and his courage all in one fell swoop.

eight

Jessa carried the mat in and shut the door behind her. It had been three days since Clint's suggestion, and even though she hadn't heard from him anymore, she'd decided to take his advice. After Seth left with his final delivery for the evening, Jessa ran down to the dollar store and bought a rolled up rectangle of bright red foam that proclaimed *Kindergartener* in proud yellow letters.

As she unrolled it and slid it carefully under her sleeping bag, she resisted the urge to try it out. She needed to wash her hair and clean up the best she could. She'd always heard of girls who stayed home on Friday nights to wash their hair, and now she was about to join their ranks. It would be a change. Usually she stayed home on Friday nights to read a book.

With a towel around her shoulders, Jessa bent over the deep sink and turned the faucet on to test the temperature. With no warning, water spurted from the faucet in every direction. She screamed and reached for the knobs, but no matter how she turned them, water continued to squirt out willy-nilly, until she was completely soaked and standing in a puddle of water. Finally, she pushed down and gave the knobs one more hard twist. The deluge stopped as suddenly as it had started. She sputtered and swiped at her eyes. A loud knock sounded on the back door.

She hadn't heard from him since Tuesday, but with his penchant for showing up unexpectedly, it could only be Clint McFadden. Heedless of the water running off her, she squished through the back room and yanked open the door.

Elaine McFadden smiled at her uncertainly. "Are you okay? I thought I heard you scream."

Speechless, Jessa nodded, then stood back and let Clint's mother in, closing the door behind her. She could feel the rivulets of water still streaming down her face.

"What happened?"

"The faucet attacked me, and I couldn't get it to stop."

Elaine took the towel from Jessa's shoulders and dabbed her face. "Should I call the police?" From anyone else, the motherly gesture would have irritated Jessa, but coupled with Elaine's pseudo-serious question, instead it struck her as funny.

Both women burst out laughing.

"If the police are coming, I'd better make myself more presentable." Jessa flipped her head over and deftly wrapped the wet towel around her dripping hair in a turban.

Elaine looked around at the small room, and Jessa followed her gaze. The tiny round table with the three books and Bible lying atop it. The rickety shelf holding the folded clothes. And the pillow and sleeping bag in the corner with the red mat peeking out precociously.

Elaine waved a hand around the room in an exaggerated gesture. "I love what you've done with the place."

They giggled again.

"Thank you, dahling. It was just something I threw together." Jessa leveled her gaze on Elaine. "With the help of a very sweet woman."

"Pshaw. You do go on." Elaine flopped one hand in the air.

"No fair. I've never actually heard anyone say 'Pshaw,'" Jessa protested.

"Me either." Elaine's blue eyes, so much like Clint's, sparkled. "But you started it with 'dahling.'"

"Guilty as charged."

"You and the water faucet, too. Maybe I *should* call the police." Elaine grinned. "You're probably wondering what I'm doing here."

"No. Telling you on the phone wasn't enough. I'm glad to get a chance to talk to you in person," Jessa said. "To let you know again how much I appreciated the wonderful things you sent." She grabbed another towel from the bathroom and padded back in to where Elaine had begun to mop water from the floor with a paper towel.

"It was fun getting the things together." Elaine stood and helped Jessa drape the extra towel around her shoulders. "But not as much fun as it would be if you'd come stay with us until you find a place."

Jessa knew in an instant that Elaine was sincere. She really would enjoy having Jessa around, and Jessa would enjoy it as well. She looked at the sleeping bag in the corner, and her hand instinctively went to her sore back. Then she touched the turban-twisted towel around her still dirty hair. If she stayed with the McFaddens for a few days, she could at least get a warm shower and sleep in a real bed.

Elaine showed no signs of wanting to take over her life. Jessa felt her stubborn streak slinking away to the corner.

"The allure of clean hair and a soft bed is more than I can resist." She smiled at Elaine. "But I promise I won't impose for more than a few days."

"Let's get you moved for now."

For the next ten minutes, they loaded everything back into the black garbage bag. Still wearing the towel on her head, Jessa carried the bag to her car, and Elaine deposited the sleeping bag, rolled mat, and pillow into the backseat.

"Follow me," she called happily, as she climbed into her SUV.

"Gladly," Jessa said under her breath, as she slid into her car.

❧

"Something smells delicious." Clint walked into the kitchen. His mom looked up from where she was slicing tomatoes and smiled. His dad carefully extracted a pan of rolls from the oven and waved them teasingly under Clint's nose.

Clint grinned. It still startled him a little to see Jeb McFadden working in the kitchen. For the first thirty-five years of their marriage, he hadn't exactly been a chauvinist, but deep down he'd definitely considered kitchen duty women's work. Since Jeb's retirement, though, Clint's mom had opened up his eyes to the joy of cooking, as well as many other things.

His mom just had a way about her. Which would explain Jessa's car in the driveway.

"Are we having company?"

Elaine shook her head. "No, just us and our houseguest."

Clint stole a dill pickle slice off her perfectly arranged plate. "You're feeling proud of yourself, aren't you?" He popped it into his mouth and when he'd finished, reached for another. His mom was too fast for him and slapped his hand with the salad spoon. "Ow!"

"As a matter of fact, I'm feeling pretty proud of Jessa. Sometimes it takes a bigger person to accept help than to refuse."

The festive mood in the kitchen grew serious for a second. His mother was the queen of unspoken references. "Uh-oh, now that you've got Jessa settled in, you're back to me." He hugged her. "I promise I'll accept help if I find any for what ails me, Mom."

"You know where to find it. You've just quit looking to the right place." She sprinkled cheddar cheese on the green lettuce.

His dad nodded, but Clint could see sympathy in his face.

Jeb understood what it felt like to be caught in Elaine's crosshairs, especially when she was dead right.

Clint shifted uncomfortably. He knew his bitter anger toward God bothered his parents. But the turmoil inside him was too great to pretend otherwise. He attended church services largely because he hated to see the worry on his parents' faces. Everything he'd counted on his whole life had shifted the day Ryan died in the fire.

"Knock, knock." Jessa's voice broke the silence in the room.

Clint stared at her as she walked in. What had happened to the cute little freckle-faced redhead with wild hair and upturned nose?

In her place stood a vision of beauty. Her strawberry blond hair was twisted up with some kind of clip, and curls cascaded down from it. He couldn't tell if she had on any makeup, but she must have, because the freckles were nowhere to be seen. And something she'd done made her eyes stand out until he thought he could get lost in them.

"Breathe, Son," his dad muttered in his ear.

"Jessa, come in." Elaine grinned at Jeb's barely perceptible comment but hurried over to make her guest feel at home.

"Is there anything I can do to help?"

"Well, let's see. . ." Elaine wiped her hands on the towel that hung on the cabinet pull and nodded. "You can put the ice in the glasses."

While she got Jessa started on her assigned task, Clint inwardly thanked his mom for giving him time to gather his thoughts.

"So, Clint?" Jessa asked over her shoulder as she divvied ice cubes into the glasses, "Did you recognize me without the ponytail?"

He grinned. Trust her to address his speechlessness head on.

"You clean up real nice."

"Thanks." She turned back to Elaine. "Nothing like begging for a compliment."

Clint smiled politely, but his pulse pounded in his ears. His career was over, his life in turmoil, his faith a wreck. Now was the worst possible time for him to meet the girl of his dreams. But his heart seemed to have a mind of its own.

nine

"Y'all just visit while I bring the dessert." Elaine stood, and Jessa started to rise too, but Clint's dad waved her back to her seat.

"No, Jessa, you're our guest tonight. I'll help her." Jeb rose and aimed a broad wink at Elaine. "She's always trying to get me alone anyway."

Clint and Jessa chuckled as the older couple left the room, still teasing each other as the door shut behind them.

"Are they always like that?"

"Always."

"You're lucky."

"Don't your parents tease?"

"Not much."

"Well, some people are just not as. . .hmm. . .exuberant as Dad and Mom." He grinned. "In case you were wondering, I was looking for a tactful word."

"They're wonderful." The easy atmosphere in the McFadden place was in stark contrast to the tense house she'd been raised in.

She'd been a little nervous about eating supper with the family because she hadn't heard from Clint since their lunch on Tuesday, but he'd acted completely normal. Her nerves had calmed as the meal had progressed.

She glanced at the mahogany mantel above the fireplace. Row after row of framed photographs lined the top. "Looks like they've raised a big family."

"Yep." He pointed to the large picture in the center.

Jessa stood and walked across the hardwood floor for a closer look.

"Just a bunch of ugly mugs, mostly," Clint joked as Jessa perused the framed photographs on the mahogany mantel. "Of course, there might be one handsome one in the bunch."

"Oh, really." She pointed at the group picture, taken when the boys were teens. "This has to be you on this end. And the other three are your brothers?"

"Yes."

"I always wanted a brother."

"There were times when I was growing up that I would have gladly given you one of mine."

Jessa chuckled. "I know what you mean. There were times I would have given you my sister, too."

Clint shook his head. "Never wanted a sister."

"I wouldn't have figured you for a woman hater."

"I don't hate women. But when I was ten, my cousin came to spend the summer." He nodded toward a blond smiling out of a small frame. "She was a girl." A mischievous glint twinkled in his eye. "A teenage girl. That was enough to sour me on ever wanting a sister."

"Do you have sisters-in-law?"

"Yep, two of them. Now, if either of them had come to stay, it would have been a different story. I'd probably have begged Mom for a sister. Or even if she'd been more like you."

His unabashed grin turned Jessa's knees to jelly, and she quickly turned back toward the mantel, leaning forward to look at the pictures in the back row.

The firefighter's yellow hat shaded his eyes in the photograph, but the crooked grin was a dead giveaway. Jessa picked up the framed snapshot and peered closer at it. Clint was a fireman.

Why hadn't he mentioned that rather important detail in all their conversations about heroes and fires? No wonder he'd sounded so positive about how to act at a fire scene when they were at the cabin the morning after.

"So, did you get settled into the guest room?" Clint spoke from behind her.

She spun around, picture still in her hand, to face Clint. "Why didn't you tell me you're a fireman?"

His smile disappeared. Knitting his brows together, he shrugged. "I'm not anymore. So, it's not worth talking about."

He wasn't anymore? The tiny red date stamp in the bottom left corner of the photo showed that it had been only two months since the picture had been taken. Curiosity prodded her to keep the subject open, but his attitude strongly discouraged further questions.

The hostile expression on his face now was a far cry from the happy smile in the photo she held. Her tongue grew dry in her mouth. Heart pounding, she turned back to the fireplace and carefully replaced the picture.

She made a show of looking over the rest of the photos. Good looks and winning smiles ran through this family like a golden thread through a tapestry. They all looked so strong and healthy.

She could feel Clint's gaze boring into her back. He was probably trying to decide if she was going to let the matter drop or not. She spun around. "Nice family."

"I like them." He wasn't frowning anymore, but his slight smile didn't reach his eyes.

Before she could reply, Elaine and Jeb entered the room each holding a tray. Elaine looked from Clint to Jessa as if she suspected tension. "I thought we might want to take our dessert and coffee out on the deck."

Clint cleared his throat. "I'm going to go on up to bed." He nodded at Jessa but didn't meet her gaze. "Hope you get settled in okay." He dropped a quick kiss on his mom's cheek. "Thanks for supper, Mom. Delicious as always."

He was gone before Elaine could respond. Jeb balanced his tray with one hand and gave his wife a reassuring squeeze on her arm with the other. "Well," he boomed, smiling at Jessa, "that'll mean more dessert for the rest of us."

Jessa returned Jeb's smile, but for all his joviality there was no denying the concern that lurked in Clint's dad's eyes.

❧

Clint stomped up the wooden steps to his apartment. Jessa Sykes got under his skin. When she had latched on to that picture of him in his uniform, he had seen the multitude of unasked questions in her eyes. It was only a matter of time before they came tumbling out.

They were questions he wasn't prepared to answer. Not for her, not for anyone.

Shame washed over him. He couldn't bear for this woman who had proclaimed him as her "hero" to know what an absolute failure he was. What would she think of him if she knew the truth? Would she still call him a "hero" if she knew he'd been unable to save his best friend when he was only a few feet away? That now he was afraid of fire?

What a laugh. A fireman afraid of fire. That would be like a teacher afraid of kids or a florist afraid of flowers. Clint flung the apartment door open. To his amazement, the yellow pup ran to him, wagging his tail.

"Hey, Rapscallion." Clint had no idea what Jessa had in mind to name the little pup, but he'd taken to calling him by the only moniker that seemed to fit. He reached out to pet the dog.

Instead of cowering and running away, the suddenly friendly canine jumped up at him. Clint looked over at the sofa and TV. He'd intended to veg out for the next several hours. To sit like he had every other night, mindlessly staring at the screen, not even knowing if it was on or not.

Rapscallion apparently had other ideas.

When Clint grabbed the leash and bent down, he barely got his head turned in time to redirect the puppy's sloppy kiss to his cheek. "Good boy." Clint rubbed the dog's nose. "Now be still." To his amazement, Rapscallion stood without moving until Clint got the leash fastened to the collar.

As he gave the puppy an affectionate hug, a sudden thought occurred to him. Now that Jessa had moved into the house, he wouldn't have any reason to keep the dog. His parents wouldn't mind Rapscallion staying with her in the guest room. He probably should take him back to her immediately.

But then again, with it being her first night in almost a week to sleep in a real bed, surely she'd rather wait until tomorrow to have to worry about taking care of a dog. Holding tightly to the leash, Clint kicked the door shut behind him.

Rapscallion scampered down the steps and bounded into the small grove of trees next to the house. When the dog reached the end of the line, he pulled up and ran back to Clint.

"You're getting used to the leash quickly, aren't you, boy?" Clint kept his voice low, mindful of Jessa and his parents still enjoying dessert around back. After he returned Rapscallion to Jessa, the apartment would once again become the lonely prison it had been.

ten

Four short hours ago, Jessa had gone to work determined to fix her faucet and get her life back on track. Since the shop was only open until noon on Saturdays, she'd been confident of having time to turn things around. But she pulled back into the driveway now, confused and worried.

Even with her frayed emotions dangling by a thread, she smiled at the sight of Clint throwing a stick for the stray pup. The man and his dog at play looked like a painting of simpler times.

She'd love someone to talk to, but after Clint's abrupt departure last night, she wasn't about to approach him. Maybe Elaine would be home. Before she could reach the door, though, his voice rang across the yard.

"Jessa!" He scooped up the puppy and waved. "Come on over."

She returned the wave. The wooden swing he motioned toward hung in the shade of a big oak tree right in front of the lake. It looked so inviting. She tossed her purse on the small patio table by the door and ambled across the yard.

She wasn't in a hurry to face Clint. From the moment he'd shown up at the hospital, her emotions had been in a jumble. The last thing she needed was a protector, but when he wasn't trying to take care of her, he had the potential to be a really good friend. Or he had, until he'd walked out before dessert last night.

She sank onto the padded cushion beside him. "Hi."

"Hey there. Since you've relocated, I thought you might want your puppy back. Mom and Dad won't mind at all." Clint sat and pushed the yellow pup toward her. The dog scrambled back into Clint's lap. Jessa watched in amazement as the puppy tucked his face behind Clint's arm with a whimper.

Clint gently stroked the dog's nose. There was no mistaking the tender regard on his face.

She gasped loudly, suppressing a grin. "Clint McFadden! You've stolen my puppy!"

He blushed and ducked his head. "He'll get used to you, too. Just give him some time." As he spoke, he rubbed the dog's shiny coat.

"I don't think I want a dog that whimpers when I try to hold it." She forced every trace of a smile from her face. "I guess I'll have to find out where the humane society building is." Truthfully, she'd never intended to keep the stray longer than it took to find him a good home, but Clint didn't have to know that. She'd give him a taste of his own teasing.

"Well, if you really don't want him. . ." His blue eyes twinkled, and she knew she hadn't fooled him for a minute. "Rapscallion will be just fine staying with me."

"Rapscallion?" She shook her head. "What kind of name is Rapscallion? I was thinking of Prince, or even Hero, after he woke me up in the fire."

"Lucky for him I'm the one naming him then, huh?"

"Lucky. . .hmm. . .that could work."

"His name is Rapscallion, and that's final." Clint pulled the puppy out from under his elbow and set him on the ground, then picked up a stick and threw it.

Jessa burst out laughing when the little dog tore after the stick, his short legs churning. When he flipped end over end, he stood, looked back at Clint, and tilted his head to first one side then the other. She laughed harder. "His name is longer than his legs."

"Watch this." Clint clapped his hands. "Come here, Rapscallion."

"That's supposed to prove he knows his name? He was halfway to you before you got the 'here' out."

Clint scooped up the excited puppy. "Everybody's a critic," he said with a rueful grin, patting the dog gently. "Good boy," he whispered.

"Seriously, I can't really have a dog right now. When I find a place to rent, chances are they won't allow pets."

"I'd love to have him then." He ruffled the pup's hair. "We understand each other."

They sat in silence for a few minutes, watching the birds fly over the placid water. She remembered how burdened she'd felt when she had gotten out of the car. What a difference a few minutes of laughter could make.

As if reading her mind, Clint cleared his throat. "You looked pretty bummed when you first got here. Everything okay?"

"I don't know. I'm tired, I guess. On Saturdays, I run the shop by myself. Doris offered to come in today because of the fire, but I told her I could handle it."

"Was it tougher than you thought?" His voice held genuine interest, but she couldn't detect even a note of pity or a hint that he thought she needed help.

"In a way. You know last night at supper when your mom and I were explaining about the deranged faucet in my shop?"

He nodded.

"Today I decided to figure out what caused my perfectly normal faucet to go off the deep end."

"And? Did you find the reason?"

"The screws on both the hot and cold handles were loose. Even though that's an awfully odd coincidence, it would explain why I had a hard time turning the water off. But that still didn't account for why the faucet itself went wild."

"So. . .being Miss Independent, instead of calling a plumber, you tore into it yourself." Clint's grin took the sting out of his words.

Jessa rolled her eyes. "That's exactly what I did. But when I unscrewed the head and took it apart, all I got was more questions."

"What do you mean?"

"There was a part missing." Before he spoke, she shook her head. "It wasn't a part that could have dissolved over time. This was a key component of the faucet. . .gone with the wind."

He smiled at her word choice. "You're not in Georgia anymore, Scarlett." But then his expression grew serious. "Why would anyone sabotage your faucet?"

"I honestly can't imagine, but there is one more thing." She quickly told him about the 'You don't belong there' phone call. "I hadn't given it another thought really until I found the faucet. It was probably just a wrong number."

"Hmm. . .maybe. If the phone call was a wrong number, and the faucet an isolated incident, could it have been a practical joke? By one of your employees?"

Jessa considered the thought of Doris playing a prank. Definitely not. And Seth barely smiled when he got his paycheck. Physical humor didn't seem his style. She shook her head. "It was working fine earlier in the day, so it had to be done while I was gone to the store. Doris had a church meeting at that time, and Seth doesn't have a key. Besides, what's the point of a prank if there's no 'gotcha!' to top it off?"

"You said you worked alone today." He ruffled Rapscallion's head but kept his gaze on Jessa. "Maybe you just haven't heard the 'gotcha' yet."

"Maybe. We'll see, I guess. Until Monday, I'm not going to worry about it." She pushed to her feet. "Right now, I've got a date with a cliff."

Clint stood. "Who's Cliff?"

"You know. Tall, rocky bluff—perfect for climbing?" Jessa blinked as the color drained from Clint's face.

"Are you kidding?"

"No, I'm serious. I joined a rock-climbing club when I first moved here." She thought the news that she would be with a group would soothe his apparently ruffled feathers, but she was wrong.

The original color came back to his face and more besides. "What? Almost dying in a burning cabin wasn't enough excitement for you this week?"

His harsh words brought quick tears to Jessa's eyes, and she jumped up to defend herself. "I didn't find anything terribly exciting about losing everything I owned and ending up in the emergency room. You've obviously never experienced the exhilaration of taking a well-planned risk."

He stared at her for a few minutes, their faces just inches apart. An incredible sadness filled his eyes, and he sank back down in the swing. He ran his hand through his hair. "Jessa, I'm so sorry. I shouldn't have said that."

"No, you shouldn't have." In spite of his apology, she couldn't keep the anger from her own voice, but she sat back down beside him.

"You don't know what it's like to face danger every day because you have to, not because you choose to. Risky sports and hobbies just seem like such a waste to me."

"And you have a right to your opinion." Jessa kept her voice level. She realized that, as a fireman, Clint had probably seen horrible things. It was natural for him to be cautious. But in that second, she also knew there was no possibility of a future for them as anything but friends. "When I'm rock climbing or kayaking or even parasailing, I feel totally alive. The danger proves that to me."

"I don't understand why you need that to make you feel alive."

His voice begged her to make him see, but she couldn't. She could never trust him with the truth. As protective as he was now, if he found out she'd ever been anything less than healthy, he'd be as bad as her family.

"Why don't you skip the climb and let me show you how exciting an afternoon of fishing on the lake can be?" Clint's crooked grin didn't reach his eyes this time. She saw desperation there instead.

Resentment boiled up inside of her. Her dad had always done that. *Jessa's not cooperating*, her mom would whisper; then her dad would put on his most cajoling smile and bribe her or offer her the moon.

Don't go out with the gang, Jessa. Look, we've hired a band and called a caterer so you can stay home with us, where you'll be safe.

She stood. "I guess we're definitely not in "The Twilight Zone" anymore. We do have original thoughts, after all. I'm going to go get ready to climb."

He nodded and stared at the ground.

Jessa walked across the yard and resisted the almost overpowering urge to look back.

&

Clint looked at the clock by his front door again. Jessa's car had pulled out of the driveway five hours ago. He'd kept himself busy while she was gone—taken Rapscallion for a run, done a couple of sets of push-ups, and taken a shower.

But, for the last thirty minutes, as dark spread across the sky, visions of her broken body at the bottom of a cliff had haunted him. Since Ryan's death, it was all too easy imagining losing someone he cared about.

The thought hit him with a jolt. Jessa was someone he cared about. But he couldn't possibly pursue a relationship with a woman who viewed risks as a way to feel alive. Especially not when he wanted to wrap her in cotton and protect her from harm.

Headlights flashed across the front window, and he peeked out. By the yellow glow of the streetlight, he recognized the blue car turning into the driveway. Relief coursed through him like a raging river. He collapsed into the overstuffed chair by the window.

He looked heavenward.

Thank You for keeping her safe.

eleven

Jessa hurried into the shop, her arms full of greenery. She'd bought extra from the delivery man today, in addition to what she'd ordered. There were two funerals tomorrow, one morning, one afternoon. Since both people had died on Sunday, the orders had flooded in this morning. With Doris out sick, Jessa had her work cut out for her.

She was glad to be occupied. It had been over three weeks since she and Clint had argued about her going rock climbing. She had seen him several times at supper, and he had been cordial, but like her, he'd kept his distance. They hadn't had one real conversation since that day.

She knew she should be happy. But her heart had ideas of its own. She missed his sense of humor and their close connection.

Shaking her head at her own foolishness, she yanked open the glass door of the cooler to place some greenery in it. To her dismay, the normally cool air was barely lower than room temperature. Her heart sank. The coolers were full of flowers.

Both coolers were the same temperature, which made no sense. They ran on different compressors. For that matter, when was the last time she'd heard either compressor kick on?

She blushed even though she was alone in the shop. Her mind puzzled on Clint so much these days that she hadn't paid any attention this morning to the sounds she knew by heart.

With a sudden feeling of dread, she squatted down and looked behind the coolers at the electrical outlet. Both plugs lay on the floor. Irritation flared up inside her. She hurriedly plugged them in and sat back on her heels as the droning compressors kicked on simultaneously.

Thank You, God, for letting me find it before the flowers were ruined.

Sabotage? Had the same person who had dismantled her faucet unplugged her coolers? Suspicions flooded in. Had Doris called in sick today so she didn't have to share responsibility for not hearing the compressors?

She forced the unpleasant thoughts from her mind and worked feverishly on the funeral sprays in between walk-in customers. Before she knew it, it was closing time. She'd managed to do all the orders for Seth to deliver to the funeral home.

When the teenager showed up, she searched his face for any indication of guilt but saw none. If he unplugged the coolers, he needed to take his acting talents to Hollywood.

"Seth, will you be seeing Ruby tonight?"

He looked up from where he was arranging the sprays in a carrier. "Probably."

"Would you tell her and Evelyn that I'll be stopping by to see them soon? I've been meaning to, but I just haven't yet."

"Sure."

After Seth left, Jessa determined that she would make more of an effort to be friendly to Clint. Maybe if she diffused the tension between them, she could get her mind back on her business, where it belonged.

❧

When Clint walked into the kitchen, his mom and Jessa had their heads together chattering like two magpies as they prepared a salad. Instead of ignoring him like she'd been doing for the past three weeks, Jessa beamed at him. His breath caught in his throat. She ought to have a license for that smile.

"Clint! Your mom has the best news. Mr. and Mrs. Anderson, next door, are leaving tomorrow to go to Florida for the winter. They won't be back until summer."

"Is that good news?" He looked at his mom. "I thought we liked the Andersons."

Jessa rolled her eyes. "That's not the good part. The house is fully furnished, and they want to rent it to me until they return, for a fraction of what it would normally cost."

Elaine reached out and wiped her hands on a towel that hung from the cabinet handle. "Actually, they would love for her to just house-sit for them, but she insisted on renting it."

That figured. Guarding her precious independence. He didn't know who had done a number on her, but it was definitely a doozy. He realized both women were waiting for his reaction. What could he say? All in all, it would probably be best if he didn't see her every day. "That's great."

His mom placed a platter of barbecued chicken in his hands, and he dutifully carried it to the table. Just as he reentered the kitchen, the cell phone clipped on his belt rang. He glanced at the caller ID, and his mind spun. It was Ryan's widow, Becky. He hadn't talked to her since the funeral.

twelve

"Mom, I have to take this call. Y'all go ahead and start without me."

He felt Jessa's gaze on him as he flipped open the phone and headed toward the back door.

"Hello?"

"Clint. How are you?"

Tears edged his eyes. He hurried off the porch and out toward the water's edge. He'd never expected to hear from her again. Not after he told her, at her insistence, what happened in the fire that had claimed her husband's life. "I'm okay. How are you?" Such a silly question, but all he could think of to say around the lump in his throat.

"I'm doing well. Still missing Ryan every day, but God is getting me through it."

Her words stabbed like a knife. She was missing her husband because Clint hadn't been able to get to him. "Is God getting you through it, Clint?" The tenderness in her voice twisted the blade. "Are you letting Him?"

"Not really." He half-sobbed, half-gasped, fighting valiantly at the tears. He'd had enough tears to last a lifetime. "I'm not real happy with Him. And I'm even less happy with myself." He put the heel of his hand against his forehead and squeezed his eyes shut.

"I wish you could understand. Ryan was ready to go. He basically told you that before he died. He always knew that was a chance he took, being a fireman." Becky's voice became thick with tears. "If he knew you lost your faith because he went home to be with God, he'd be devastated. He loved you like a brother."

"I loved him, too. I'm sorry, Becky. I tried to get to him." His sobs were shaking him now. He couldn't stop them.

"I know that. But he's waiting for us. And you can't live your life if you keep blaming yourself. Everyone knows there was nothing you could have done."

"What about God? If He's so mighty, couldn't He have done something?"

"Clint." Becky sounded disappointed in him, and it was almost more than he could bear. "You know the Bible says that everyone has a time to go. It was Ryan's time. God's ways aren't for us to understand. But we know they work together for good for those of us who love Him. And no matter what you think right now, I know you do love Him."

He broke in. "Beck, I really can't talk about it right now. I love you, but I just can't. I'll call you soon." He flipped the phone shut and lay back on the grass, gulping air into his lungs, which burned like he'd run ten miles. For a long time he gazed at the starry sky. What was wrong with him that Ryan's loving widow could go on with her life, but he couldn't?

❧

Saturday dawned bright and sunny, and Jessa murmured a prayer of thanks. When Doris had offered to take care of the shop today so she could move, Jessa had gratefully taken her up on it.

She'd opted to load things into her car and drive them around rather than track across the dewy grass. Sadly, she thought, she could get everything in one trip. Her old landlord had insisted that the things Jessa had stored in the shed were fine there indefinitely, and since the Andersons had their own summer things in their shed, Jessa really had no choice.

Jeb and Elaine had left early to drive to St. Louis for the day. Their youngest son was a pitcher for the Cardinals and had a home game today. Jessa packed her clothes in the two suitcases Elaine had loaned her for that purpose and lugged them out to the car.

"Hey." Clint stood at the edge of the driveway with Rapscallion on a leash. "You moving out?"

"Yep."

He looked at the sky. "Nice weather for moving."

"Yep." She cringed. Had she forgotten to wake her vocabulary this morning? "I'm thankful."

When she had just finished packing the plastic tub with her toiletries, Clint appeared in the doorway. "Need any help?"

"You're a little late now," she said tartly, then immediately regretted it.

Without speaking, he lifted the plastic tub, carried it to her car, and loaded it in the trunk. She followed behind him with her pillow and trusty sleeping bag. "I think that's it."

"I'll walk over and help you unload."

"Okay."

As she drove the short distance to the next driveway, she mused on the odd turn of events. Maybe they would manage to be friends without wanting more. It would certainly be nice if they could.

Thirty minutes later Clint carried the last load in. "While you unpack, why don't I run to the store and get some charcoal and steaks? You deserve a housewarming celebration after all you've been through."

Jessa nodded. "That sounds fun."

After Clint left, Jessa examined the house that would be

her home for the next several months. Considerably more modest than the McFaddens but still much larger and newer than the cabin, it was just right for her. It had been really nice of Clint to think of celebrating.

Just as she finished putting everything away, he knocked on the back door.

"Just wanted you to know I've got the grill going." His crooked smile once again lit up his normally brooding face. "And I've brought a few things to go with the steak." He handed her a plastic grocery bag.

"Oh, good." She peeked in at the salad fixings and frozen cheese toast. "Great! I'll go get them ready."

"Give me a five-minute head start on the steaks."

"Will do." As she hurried into the kitchen, her spirits soared. She had high hopes she would be able to be friends with Clint McFadden without any complications.

When they sat down to eat, she turned to her guest. "Will you offer thanks for our food?"

His face turned red, but he nodded. "Dear God, Thank You for this food. Please bless Jessa in her new home. In Jesus' name. Amen."

"I'm sorry if I made you uncomfortable."

"No, that's okay." He fiddled with his fork for a minute, then looked back up. "I'm not on very good terms with God right now. But I'm working on it."

She nodded. That explained the brooding eyes. "Thank you for your prayer."

"You're welcome."

She tasted the steak and closed her eyes. "Mmm. . .you are a wonderful chef."

He laughed. "Don't let my brothers hear you say that. We'll have more grilled meat than we know what to do with.

It's kind of a competition between us."

"Well, you would win."

"I'll make sure you're a judge next time we all get together." He grinned. "By the way, I've been wondering. Did you ever have any more incidents like your broken faucet? Besides the phone call?"

She nodded. "Actually, yes. Monday afternoon I discovered that both coolers were unplugged. There's no way that could have been an accident. Two separate plug-ins."

"Did you call the police?"

"No. I know, I know. I probably should." She poured a liberal dollop of ranch dressing on her salad. "But I just feel silly. Nothing was hurt. I found them in time to save the flowers."

"Do you like a little salad with your dressing?"

"Hey!" She put her arms protectively around her plate. "At my house, we're not allowed to talk about each other's eating habits."

"At your house, huh? You're pretty proud, aren't you?"

"Yes, I am. And you had the honor of being the first friend I had over."

"Sure, sure, but I had to help carry things and cook the meal to get invited. I'm not sure what kind of deal that is."

"Well, if I'd have known you were such a complainer, I'd have asked someone else."

ช

An hour later, Clint picked up the Frisbee and flung it to Jessa. She jumped to catch it, but Rapscallion leaped for the flying disc at the same time, and they went tumbling to the ground together.

Clint ran to her. "Are you okay?"

She sat up laughing, then frowned at the worried expression

in his eyes. "Yes, I'm fine. You might want to check on your dog though. I think he cushioned my blow."

Clint stared at her a moment, then chuckled. "I'll get you for animal cruelty if you don't stop throwing your weight around."

Rapscallion, seemingly anxious to prove his good health, grabbed the Frisbee and took off across the yard. Jessa jumped up and, taking the challenge, ran after him. But within seconds, he ran behind Clint's leg and barked at her from his safe haven.

She pulled up short, right in front of Clint, gasping for air.

"Whoa, there." Clint reached out an arm to steady her.

She leaned against him without thinking. He brought his other arm around her, and she relaxed, the tension of the last few weeks draining from her.

"I've missed you." His voice was husky with emotion.

"Same here." She looked up at him.

His blue eyes darkened. Just as he lowered his lips to hers, Rapscallion leaped up between them, barking wildly.

She jumped back. Clint bent down and clipped the dog's leash on him. When he stood, his penetrating gaze seemed to see into her soul. "I'd better go."

"Yeah. Thanks for coming. The steaks were great."

He nodded and led the dog across the short expanse of grass that joined the two backyards.

Her legs trembled as she walked into the house.

thirteen

The next morning, his emotions still in turmoil, Clint see-sawed back and forth about going to church. Just as the service began, he slid into the back pew. He turned to murmur an apology for disturbing the person next to him and looked straight into the greenest eyes in the whole county.

Who ever said God didn't have a sense of humor?

She smiled. A knot in his stomach loosened. For the next hour, he put Ryan's death from his mind and concentrated on the worship.

As they walked out into the unseasonably warm September day, she tucked her arm in the crook of his elbow. "Do you have somewhere you need to go right now?"

"No." He had planned to sit in his apartment and mope all afternoon, but that was nothing that couldn't be canceled.

"Let's go home, get changed, and go out for a drive. We need to talk."

"Okay." He kept his answer short so she wouldn't hear the apprehension in his voice. He'd never heard of a conversation that began with "We need to talk" that ended well.

Once home, he quickly let Rapscallion out and then changed into jeans and a T-shirt. He walked out to the swing to wait for her, a sudden idea niggling at his mind.

❧

"Fishing?" Jessa laughed. "Sure, why not?"

She had known this morning when she was sitting on the pew beside Clint that she had to be completely honest with him. She'd never been a game player, and she wasn't about to start now.

Out on the lake would be a fine place to tell him. At least that way if he got upset by her decision, he couldn't run off before they finished talking.

Thirty minutes later, they sat in Jeb's small fishing boat in the middle of Lake Millicent.

"Now what?"

"Depends." He raised an eyebrow. "On whether you want to fish first and talk later or talk first and fish later."

"We'd better fish first," she said. "Then maybe we can talk during."

"Fine with me." Clint handed her an artificial lure, and she slid the brightly colored bait onto the hook. "Too bad we didn't have time to dig some worms."

"Yeah." She shuddered. "Too bad."

She followed the careful instructions he gave her and raised the tip of her rod up in the air then slung it forward. The baited hook and sinker slammed into the side of the boat.

"You forgot to take your thumb off the button as you cast. Here, let me show you." He stood gingerly in the boat and leaned over her chair, putting both arms around her and placing his hand on hers.

He smelled of soap, the kind that reminded her of a crisp breeze across the ocean. She shivered. He could surely hear her heartbeat. It sounded like a tribe of angry cannibals banging on the tom-tom drums.

"You cold?" His voice was right next to her ear, and she could feel the warmth of his breath on her skin.

"No. Just ready to get started." She knew her tone was short, but this talk wasn't going quite like she planned.

He lightly pushed down on her thumb. With gentle hands, he guided her to bring the reel back and then forward in one fluid motion, releasing the button just as she began the downward stroke. Her hook went flying through the air and plopped thirty feet from the boat.

He took his arms from around her and sank into his seat again, then quickly repeated the move with his own rod.

She stared out at the water and tried to forget how right it felt to have his arms around her, even if it was just for a casting lesson. They sat in silence for a few minutes. Jessa's mouth grew dry with words unspoken.

"Was there something in particular you wanted to talk about?" Clint spoke softly, but his voice carried across the deserted water.

Unable to face him, she swiveled her seat away from him slightly. "Yes."

"I'm all ears."

"There's no easy way to say this."

"Whatever it is, I can about guarantee you I'll understand. Just pretend we're back in The Twilight Zone."

Tears sprang to her eyes at his kind words. She chuckled. "Okay, here goes. When I was five years old, my little brother died of a ruptured appendix. My parents, as well as my older sister and I, were devastated." Her throat ached with unshed tears.

"I'm sorry."

She nodded, still refusing to turn toward Clint. "Right after my sixth birthday, I started not feeling well. My parents, already understandably overprotective, took me to the doctor." Here it was. The part that would irrevocably change how he looked at her. "I had leukemia. My parents were sure I was going to die. I almost did. I spent the next three years in and out of the hospital, but when I was nine, the doctors pronounced the leukemia completely gone."

"Thank You, God." Clint's prayer was simple, but his spontaneous words broke the dam that had held Jessa's tears back.

She nodded, hot tears splashing down her cheeks, and tried to concentrate on the soothing ripple of the water.

"If it had ended there, that would have been a wonderful thing. To look death in the face for three years and come out perfectly healthy. But it didn't end there."

"The cancer came back?" Tension laced Clint's question.

She shook her head. "No. I've been cancer free for seventeen years." She held her rod and reel in one hand and swiped at her tears with the other. "But from that point on, my parents took protectiveness to a whole new level. They didn't want me out of their sight. When they couldn't watch me, they goaded my sister to report what I ate, what I drank, whether I was feverish. . ." The words, pent up so long, tumbled out now as she held nothing back. "I couldn't go out with friends or do anything because they were afraid they'd lose me. . .even after I became an adult."

"Besides being miserable, I'm sure you felt really guilty."

She spun around in her chair. "Guilty?" How could he possibly know that? She'd never told anyone about the guilt.

"Well, it was natural for you to feel guilty when your brother died and you didn't, and then when you got sick, because your parents loved you so much but all you wanted was to get away from them. To deprive them of another child."

"How did you get to be so smart?"

"Psychology major."

She was as shocked as she had been when she'd found the firefighter picture.

He smiled. "Yes, it's a classic case of 'Physician, heal thyself.'"

She waited for him to expound, certain his comment had to do with whatever had caused a psychology major/firefighter to end up living in his parents' garage apartment and working for lake security. But apparently, he decided one gut-wrenching confession was enough, because he just reeled his line in and cast it out again.

Finally she spoke. "You're probably wondering why I told you all that."

"Well," he drawled, "I'd like to think it's because we're friends, but I figure there's more to it than that."

He gave her that all-too-familiar grin, and she had to push the words past the lump that rose in her throat. "Clint, you're a wonderful person. And I hope we can stay friends."

He smacked his forehead with his palm. "I can't believe I wasted my best fishing tackle for a 'let's be friends' talk."

She giggled and felt the tension release. "You know what I mean. I've worked too hard to become independent. My parents haven't changed a bit, and I can't move halfway across the country to get away from that and end up involved with a protector."

He arched his eyebrow. "Didn't you ever hear you're not supposed to label people? What exactly do you consider a 'protector'?"

She rolled her eyes. "A protector—someone who doesn't want me to rock climb, doesn't want me to parasail."

"Oh, I get it. . . You mean someone with good sense."

"Now wait a minute—"

He held up his hand. "Only kidding."

He rose quickly from his seat and wrapped his arms around her. Her heart skipped several beats. "Clint," she croaked. "I meant it about being friends."

He dropped a kiss on her forehead. "Friends don't let friends lose perfectly good fish," he said dryly as he put his hand on hers and guided her in reeling in her catch.

An hour later as they rowed back to the shore, she tried to understand what had happened. She'd poured out her secrets in the hopes of confining their relationship within safe parameters. To her dismay, the resistance was coming from the wrong side.

Clint seemed perfectly satisfied with being friends, but every time he was near, her traitorous heart longed for more.

fourteen

On Monday afternoon, Doris left a few minutes early to pick up her granddaughter from school, so Jessa was alone when Seth came in.

"Hi, Jessa. How's it going?" His slight smile was a pleasant change from the almost sullen boy who had first started working for her. Maybe her efforts to draw him out were paying off. She felt a connection with him that was hard to explain.

"I'm doing pretty good. Remember a week or so ago when you couldn't believe I'd never been fishing?"

He nodded.

"Well, I have now. Clint took me yesterday afternoon, and I caught one."

A glimmer of interest flickered in his eyes. "What kind?"

"Well, you'd have to ask Clint. It was actually kind of ugly."

"What lake did you go on? Millicent?"

She nodded. "Have you ever been out on it?"

"Naw." He ducked his head. "You have to be a resident or a guest to fish on those lakes."

Jessa could see the longing in his eyes.

"Where do you live?"

He blushed and named a part of town that she recognized as the poorest section of Lakehaven.

Big mouth, she scolded herself silently. "Well, we'll have to make that our goal. To get you out on Lake Millicent."

"No biggie." He picked up the flower carrier and carefully

loaded the bouquets in it. "I don't have much time to fish anyway."

Afraid of saying the wrong thing, she nodded and held the door open for him.

After Seth was gone, she wiped off the already clean counter and made a quick check through the front room for trash or anything out of place.

She looked up at the big clock. A few minutes after five. Clint should be off work.

She snorted with self-disgust. She'd thought of him more since she'd given him the "let's be friends" talk, as he called it, than before. She couldn't believe she'd explained to him that they could only be friends when he'd never really expressed any interest in being anything more. He'd probably been secretly relieved.

She shook her head. This line of thought was getting her nowhere fast. It was time to go home. She grabbed her purse and unlocked the back door.

A loud crash resounded through the building. She dropped her purse and ran into the front room, then slammed her hand to her mouth. Four of her most expensive silk arrangements lay on the floor, the vases shattered to smithereens. She stepped forward, being careful of the shards of glass.

"Jessa? What happened?"

She jumped and spun around.

Clint stood in the doorway, still in his Tri-Lake security uniform.

"I'm not sure. I unlocked the back door and was about to leave, then I heard the crash."

Clint stepped up closer to examine the wall where minutes before a wooden shelf had supposedly been securely anchored to the wall.

"Come here and let me show you something." He reached out his hand to guide her around the glass.

He pointed at two places where chunks of drywall had come out, apparently with the screws that had held the shelf. "Now look at these."

Slightly to the right of each of those places was a small hole with a metal wall anchor in it.

"Someone moved the shelf?"

"It sure looks that way." He reached to the shelf above the one that fell and handed her a big vase with silk flowers. "Set these on the counter."

When they had transferred the last arrangement to the counter, Clint gently pulled on the wooden board. The shelf easily came loose from the wall, just like the first one, taking pieces of Sheetrock with it.

She gasped. Clint nodded grimly, carefully setting the shelf down on the floor away from the broken mess. He methodically went through the remaining seven shelves and discovered three more had been tampered with.

Jessa got the broom and dustpan and began to clean up the broken glass.

"Aren't you going to call the police?"

"And tell them what? That my shelf fell?" She shook her head and went back to sweeping.

"I still think it would be a good idea. Just to alert them to a possible problem." He reached around the counter and retrieved the small garbage can.

"You think more things will happen?" She kneeled down and picked up the biggest pieces, dropping them into the trashcan.

He squatted down next to her. "Be careful. You'll cut yourself."

She looked up at him.

He regarded her intently. "That was a 'protector' thing to say, huh?"

She nodded.

"Sorry. Anyway, back to your question. Do I think more things will happen?" He shook the glass off the silk flowers down into the garbage, then laid them in a pile to the side. "Remember the faucet?"

"Yeah."

He nodded at the mess they were cleaning up. "Same person."

"Does psychological profiling tell you that?"

"Nope." He stood. "Common sense tells me that." He pulled a multipurpose tool from his pocket and flipped out a screwdriver.

He carefully put each bracket screw back into the wall anchors. Jessa handed him the shelves one at a time until they were all back in place. The extra length covered the small holes in the drywall, but Jessa knew they were there.

Clint helped her divide the remaining arrangements between the empty shelves. When they finished, it was difficult to even see that anything had happened.

"So who can it be?" Jessa asked, hoping against hope she was wrong.

"You tell me."

"You think it has to be one of my two employees, don't you?"

Clint nodded grimly. "It looks that way."

"I don't like that theory. Let's explore the whole intruder idea."

He looked up at the ceiling. "She'd rather have an intruder than a dishonest employee."

She punched him on the shoulder. "You know what I

mean. Could someone have come in and done this?"

"Not without a key. No sign of forced entry."

"Whoa, you just started the job and already you sound like security."

"Yeah, that's me, jack of all trades, master of none."

"I don't know, it seems to me like you're good at everything you do." As soon as the words were out, her face grew hot. She always seemed to open her mouth without thinking when he was around.

"I appreciate the vote of confidence. You may take it back when I tell you that Seth is my chief suspect."

"He doesn't have a key."

"There are ways around that. A window left unlatched, or even slipping back and unlocking the front door after you'd already checked it."

She thought of the sixteen-year-old boy she was growing closer to every day. Admittedly she didn't know him well, but she liked him. And he'd done nothing to make her think he wasn't worthy of her trust. "Oh, Clint, I don't want it to be Seth. He's had a hard life. I was going to ask you to take him fishing."

"That might not be a bad idea. He might admit to it."

She put her hands on her hip. "I didn't mean so you could interrogate him. I meant so he could enjoy what we enjoyed yesterday."

He fixed her with an inscrutable gaze. "What did we enjoy yesterday?"

She refused to rise to the bait. "I mean the beauty of God's creation, the peace of being on the lake. He's not a bad kid, Clint. I'm just sure of it."

"I hope you're right. But somebody is guilty."

Jessa looked around the room. Unless a person was familiar

with the inventory, like she and Doris were, they wouldn't realize anything had even happened.

"Thanks again." She waved her hand at the clean room. "Glad I could help." He put the trash can back where he'd gotten it; then he helped her turn the lights off.

In the parking lot, she turned to face him. "Thank you again for helping me clean up that mess."

"No problem."

When she got into her car, she noticed he waited in his Jeep until she pulled out of the driveway, then eased onto the road behind her.

Ever the protector.

Why did she feel all warm and fuzzy instead of defensive?

❧

"Skinny's has nothing on you, Jessa." Clint popped the last bite of the sandwich in his mouth. "That was wonderful."

"Thanks. I have a confession, though." Jessa picked up the sandwich wrappers and plates and tucked them neatly in the basket.

"Sounds interesting. Let's hear it." He took a sip of tea. He'd been shocked to find Jessa waiting at his Jeep when it was time for his lunch break. It had been three days since he'd helped her repair the shelves. He hadn't seen her since except for a glimpse of her in her car now and then.

"I fixed lunch for you because I need a sounding board. I think Doris may be behind the accidents." Jessa's voice rose. "I know you think it's Seth, but that's because Doris didn't have a motive, but now Doris does have a motive. So you can't think that anymore—"

"Whoa, slow down there." He held up a hand. "I didn't know a Georgia peach could drawl that fast. Now what makes you think Doris has a motive for sabotaging the shop?"

"This morning I was in the back room when a customer came in. I wasn't eavesdropping. . ." She looked intently at him, as if to be sure he understood that. "But I couldn't help but overhear. The woman asked Doris what had happened to her idea of buying the shop, and Doris told her she just couldn't work out the financing." Jessa's voice trembled.

"Hmm. . ." Clint frowned. It did sound incriminating. "So was that all Doris said?"

"No, she said she guessed it just wasn't God's will for her right now. But she could have just been saying that because she knew I could hear her." Her words still tumbled over one another. Obviously the sabotage had upset Jessa even more than she admitted.

"Or it could have been the truth."

She ran her fingers through her hair, and tears glistened in her green eyes. "I don't know what to think."

"Me, either. But I do know that as much as I like Seth, he's hiding something. I can see it in his eyes."

"That just makes no sense."

"Nothing about this does." He glanced at his watch. His lunch hour was almost up. He got to his feet and offered a hand to Jessa.

She put her hand in his, and he helped her to her feet.

"So what do I do?" She didn't jerk her hand away. Her eyes pleaded for answers. Answers he didn't have.

He pulled her into his arms. She relaxed against him, and he brushed her hair with his hand. "Just keep praying. God will help you figure it out."

She leaned up on tiptoes and touched his cheek with her lips. "Thanks, Clint. See you soon." She threw the blanket over her arm and grabbed the picnic basket. She was halfway to the car before he realized she was gone.

Staring after the red-haired bundle of energy, he put his hand to his cheek. When had she become such an integral part of his life?

fifteen

Jessa's heart pounded as she slid into the car. She couldn't believe she'd kissed him. At least she'd settled for his cheek. Even though she'd made a quick getaway, she sensed he had reacted as strongly as she had to their embrace. He still stood at their picnic spot staring this way.

Dear God, please help me get this mystery figured out so I can have a clear mind to think about my feelings for this exasperating man.

She drove slowly to the shop and—other than the day after the fire—for the first time since she'd bought the shop, she entered The Flower Basket with a heavy heart.

All of Doris's kindnesses flooded back to her. And then, just as quickly, she thought of the changes in Seth's attitude, the easy camaraderie they were developing. Neither of them would hurt her like this. It just wasn't possible.

Jessa had told Doris about the mishaps with the faucet and the coolers right after they'd happened in order to see her expression. She'd seemed genuinely dismayed. There had been no hiding the fact that several silk arrangements had been broken either. Jessa had seen the pieces click together in Doris's eyes when she told her about the shelf falling. There was no doubt that the woman knew now that Jessa suspected sabotage.

Doris was carefully putting the finishing touches on an elegant fall arrangement when Jessa walked in.

"Hi," the older woman said with a smile. "Did you have a good lunch?"

"Yes, I did." Jessa decided to go around the subject and see what happened. She turned to the double coolers and began to pull the flowers out in bunches and snip the ends off the stems, something that had to be done occasionally to keep them fresh. "Can you believe all the little accidents we've been having?" She didn't look at Doris, instead concentrating completely on the flowers she held.

"No, I can't. But I've been praying that the store will be a success in spite of them."

Now what did she say to that? Jessa nodded. "Thanks," she mumbled, shame soaking through her like the bitter cold of winter.

When Jessa finished trimming the stems and had all the flowers back in the coolers, she pulled out some of her brightest-colored flowers and made an arrangement. After she tied the big red ribbon around the vase, she cleared her throat. "Doris, I'm going to run out for a little bit. I'll be back."

"No problem."

Jessa hurried out to her car.

"Knock, knock." Jessa tapped on the screen door of the small apartment Evelyn and Ruby shared. A delicious aroma floated through the screen, and her stomach growled.

"Why, Jessa! I'm so glad you stopped by. Come in, come in." Evelyn pushed the door open and held it wide enough for Jessa to enter with the large vase in her hands. "Oh, look at the lovely flowers. Ruby!" The gray-haired woman called over her shoulder. "Come see what Jessa has brought." She took the bouquet and set it on the small table in the break-fast nook.

Ruby bustled out of the kitchen. "What beautiful flowers." Jessa had only met Ruby a few times during the process of buying the shop. But she seemed like an older version of

Evelyn, and Jessa loved her already. "How did you know flowers are my favorite thing?"

Evelyn laughed and Ruby joined her. Jessa grinned. "A little birdie told me."

"Birdies are smarter these days than they used to be, aren't they, Ev?"

"They sure are. Jessa, dear, come in and have a cookie." She ushered Ruby and Jessa into the cozy kitchen. "I just took them out of the oven."

Jessa smiled at her former neighbor. "I've been eating cookies in your kitchen for over twenty years, Ev. This feels almost like I'm back in Georgia again."

Ruby turned to Jessa with a conspiratorial whisper that easily carried to Evelyn's ears. "She thinks her cookies are better than mine. But that's okay. I humor her."

Evelyn rolled her eyes. "Oh, Rube, just because you beat me in that cookie contest at the county fair. . .you always want to make the cookies now. Well, it was my turn today."

"Mighty handy that you happened to cook them on the day company showed up." Ruby scooped three cookies off the plate Evelyn extended to Jessa.

Jessa took two and accepted the glass of milk Evelyn quickly poured.

Ruby leaned over toward Jessa. "Her cookies don't dunk like mine do. If you try to dunk these, they fall apart in the milk. Mine have more staying power."

Jessa nodded. "I'll just eat them without dunking."

"Yes, do, dear. Wouldn't want to hurt Ev's feelings."

"Oh, no. . ." Evelyn drawled. "We wouldn't want to do that." She smiled at Ruby. "Besides, her cookies really are better."

"They are not! I was just pulling your leg."

Every time Jessa thought the Trent sisters were serious in

their funny bickering, they'd say or do something to show how much they loved each other.

Jessa took a deep breath. As much as she hated to bring up an unpleasant subject, she needed to find out if Ruby completely trusted Seth and Doris.

"Some things have been happening at the shop."

Ruby looked up. "At the shop?"

"What do you mean?" Evelyn asked.

"Well, accidents."

As soon as Jessa said the word *accident*, worry flitted across Evelyn's face. Jessa cringed. Her family had influenced Evelyn more than she wanted to believe. *Protect Jessa at all costs.*

"What kind of 'accidents'?" Evelyn asked.

"Oh, just little things, really, but annoying." As she began to list the incidents, they sounded almost silly.

Evelyn glanced at her watch.

"Jessa, I'm so sorry to do this. But we're going to be late for shuffleboard if we don't go right now." She blushed. "Richard counts on me being there." She reached over and squeezed Jessa tightly. "Call me tonight and we'll talk."

"Thanks for the flowers," Ruby called as Evelyn ushered Jessa to the door.

As Jessa drove back to the shop, she marveled at the twists and turns of life. After being widowed for twenty years, Evelyn had met a man. And not just any man, but one that could make her hurry Jessa out of her kitchen.

ta

"Do you think we have enough?" Seth knelt in the dirt, enthusiastically digging while Clint prepared their rod and reels.

Clint glanced down at the bucket full of squirming night crawlers. "Looks like it."

Seth stood and grabbed the metal bucket by the handle.

"Ready?" Excitement twinkled in his eyes.

"Yep. Let's go catch us a mess of fish."

As they paddled away from the shore, Clint wondered again how he'd ended up taking the boy fishing. He knew the answer in one word. Jessa. She'd pleaded until he really had no choice.

He knew one thing for certain. If his own life weren't so messed up, he wouldn't let her 'just friends' talk stop him from trying to change her mind. But as it was, common sense told him that was the only way it could be. A man living. . .make that existing. . .in his parents' garage apartment and barely on speaking terms with God had no business falling in love. No matter how wonderful she was or how lethal her smile.

Normally he wouldn't have minded taking Seth fishing either, but with his tangled life, he wasn't a role model by any stretch of the imagination. But thanks to the powers of persuasion and persistence of his red-haired *friend*, he was going to spend an afternoon making small talk with a teenager with no distractions.

Once they were in his favorite fishing spot, he looked over at Seth. "What grade are you in?"

"Tenth." The boy blushed. "Should be eleventh, but I missed too many days in fourth grade, so I failed."

"Oh, man. That must have been tough."

"Yeah, but it's okay. Most people don't realize it now."

So much for small talk, Clint thought as the silence stretched across the water.

He wordlessly handed the boy a reel and suppressed a grin when Seth expertly cast out. This boy was definitely a fisherman. Clint tossed his line several feet from Seth's. They sat for several minutes without speaking.

"I heard you were a fireman. Is that right?" Seth had apparently decided to pick up the conversational ball, unaware he'd just lobbed a bomb instead.

"Yeah, I was. But not anymore."

"Did something bad happen?"

Clint nodded shortly. "Yeah, a buddy of mine died in a fire."

"Oh. Sorry."

Even though his reply was brief, Clint could tell the boy meant it. In Seth's eyes, Clint saw a wisdom way beyond his years.

"Thanks for bringing me out here. I've always wanted to fish these lakes."

"No problem." Clint found himself fervently sharing Jessa's hope that this vulnerable boy hadn't sabotaged her shop.

"Where do you usually fish?"

He named a stream that ran through the lower part of Lakehaven, hardly more than a muddy ditch. Clint nodded. "Do you catch many?"

"Usually enough for supper."

"I bet your mom's glad of that."

"Naw. My mom died when I was born."

Well, aren't we just a barrel of laughs, Clint thought. *All of our conversations seem to lead to heartache.*

"I'm really sorry."

"Yeah, me, too. It was rough for a while, but me and my dad—we do all right now."

"Good."

Just then Seth's line grew taught. He set the hook with a jerk and began to reel frantically. Excitement sparkled in his eyes. Clint grabbed the net and opened the live well. He usually just threw his fish back in the water, but if the boy and his dad wanted them for supper, he wasn't going to argue with that.

"Whoa! It looks like a big one," Clint said, holding the net ready.

The shiny tail flashed near the surface of the water, and Clint scooped it in. Seth grinned. "She's beautiful, isn't she?"

"She sure is."

His own rod gave a yank, and he left Seth to unhook the fish and drop it in the live well. Seconds later, he reeled in one almost as big.

"Seth, buddy, I think our luck has changed."

For the next hour, they caught one fish after another. Seth's face glowed.

"Do you have enough room in your freezer for these?"

Seth nodded, grinning. "We sure do."

"Then you might as well take them all. My mom and dad have their freezer full."

"You live with your parents?"

"Just temporarily. In their garage apartment," his pride made him add.

"Oh. Bet you'll be glad to get a place of your own."

When they got back to shore, Seth refused Clint's offer to help him clean their catch. Clint felt sure the boy wanted to show them to his dad in all their glory before they were prepared for eating.

After Seth left, his last comment lingered in Clint's mind. It wasn't like he couldn't afford a house. He'd made some smart investments and had a tidy nest egg. It couldn't hurt to look.

He drove around the lake until he came to a house with a For Sale sign in the yard. It reminded him of a gingerbread cottage, and he drove on by. But the second one for sale, which appeared to be vacant, fairly screamed, 'Home!'

The well-kept cypress and rock ranch-style house appeared to have a full basement. Plenty of room for a Ping-Pong table or a playroom. He pushed the image of redheaded children from his mind and walked around to the back. As he stood looking at the backyard, which sloped gently toward the sparkling water, his heart longed for a home.

He shook his head. No matter how many houses he bought, until he made peace with his Father, there would be no home for him.

sixteen

Jessa hurried in the back door of The Flower Basket. She and Clint had met for lunch at Skinny's, and she'd hated to leave until he had to. Their friendship was developing nicely as long as they kept the boundaries well-defined. "I'm back." She grabbed an apron off the hook by the door and tied it on as she walked into the front. Doris stood staring at a vase full of flowers, shaking her head.

"Where did those come from?" Jessa asked. The bouquet looked to be at least a month old. The once red roses were shriveled and black.

"Mr. Simmons brought them in." Doris's voice held a note of incredulity.

"Why?"

"He ordered them yesterday for his wife. It was their anniversary. He said they looked fine when Seth brought them, but by the time his wife got home from the hairdresser, this is all he had to offer her." Doris reached out to touch a black petal, and it plummeted to the countertop.

Jessa put her hand to her mouth. "Oh, no." She ran behind the counter and grabbed the order pad. She stopped suddenly and turned to Doris. The older woman's eyes were wide and worry lined her face. "Doris, I hate to ask you this. Please forgive me."

Doris nodded, and Jessa thought she knew what was coming.

"Did you have anything to do with this?"

Doris shook her head. "No, I certainly didn't. I don't blame you for asking, though."

Jessa tossed her the order pad. "Thank you for that. I need your help. We have to call everyone on this pad and find out if all the flowers did this or just Mr. Simmons's order. Maybe it was a fluke." At the hope in Doris's eyes, she shook her head. "But usually if one customer complains, ten others just take their business elsewhere."

Thirty minutes later, the two women looked at each other grimly. Every bouquet they had prepared yesterday and today had died. It made no difference whether they were delivered or picked up, so that let Seth off the hook.

"What could all those flowers have come in contact with?" Jessa said.

"The water in the cooler pots?" Doris guessed.

"Some of those flowers have been in there a lot longer than hours. If that was the case, they'd die whether we put them into bouquets or not."

Doris absently tied a bow around the bouquet she'd just finished. She picked up the spray bottle of stay-fresh solution, aptly called Crowning Glory, and put her finger on the trigger.

"Wait!" Jessa reached toward Doris's hand. "That's it. Someone has tampered with the Crowning Glory."

Doris's hand froze on the spray bottle. Seth sauntered in the door. Jessa and Doris both gaped at him, and he held up his hands. "Whoa. What's up with y'all?"

The direct approach had worked so well with Doris that Jessa didn't know why she hadn't thought of it a month ago. She guessed today's prank was so far beyond a practical joke that it motivated her to act.

"We have a problem." She kept her eyes on Seth as she slid the dead bouquet over in front of him. "Those are the roses you delivered yesterday to Mr. Simmons."

Seth wrinkled his forehead. "What happened?"

Jessa stepped toward him and held his gaze. "Seth, did you tamper with the liquid we spray on the flowers to keep them fresh?"

He shook his head. "No way."

"Did you do anything to make the flowers wilt quickly?"

"No." Sincerity shone in his eyes. "I wouldn't do that."

Jessa's stomach flip-flopped. She wasn't sure if it was from the relief of knowing that neither of her employees had betrayed her or dismay that an outsider was sabotaging her business.

She nodded. "I'm sorry I had to ask you that, Seth."

"That's okay. I understand."

Doris clapped her hands together lightly. "We've got a lot of work to do." She motioned toward the table. "Since we don't have any deliveries to make right now, Seth, you can help us work up replacement bouquets for the orders from today first and then yesterday." She looked at Jessa, who nodded, grateful for someone else to take charge for a change.

"When we finish, we'll split them up by area, and all three take some. We'll get them all delivered before suppertime that way." Again she looked at Jessa, who smiled.

"I really appreciate y'all pitching in."

Seth gingerly picked up the sprayer bottle. "So you think this has poison in it?"

Jessa took it from him and unscrewed it, then put her nose to it. It had a slight chemical smell, different from the usual odor. "Yes, it looks that way." She put it over to the side. "If I decide to call the police, that'll be evidence."

At ten minutes after five, Doris and Seth left with their

deliveries. Just as Jessa was finishing her last arrangement, Clint walked in.

"What are you doing working so late?" He crossed the room and reached up to touch her hair.

Her breath caught in her throat, but he barely touched her hair, then handed her a tiny sprig of greenery. "When I saw your car in the parking lot, I was afraid something was wrong." He nodded toward all the flower arrangements lined up on the counter. "Where's Seth?"

"Seth and Doris each took five and left. These are for me to deliver."

"Is this a new marketing ploy? Canvas the neighborhood with delivered bouquets whether they're ordered or not?"

"Not exactly."

She filled him in on the afternoon's events, and he listened in concerned silence.

"So both Doris and Seth denied it, and you believe them?"

"Yes." She fiddled with the ribbon on the counter. Would he trust her gut instinct?

"That's good enough for me." He put his hand over hers. "I know you don't want to, but you need to call the police."

"You're probably right." Struggling to breathe with his thumb lightly caressing her hand, she shrugged. Apparently he'd decided to play outside the boundaries. "Seth said y'all had a fantastic time fishing. He was really excited, Clint. Thank you for taking him."

"I enjoyed it."

He released her hand, and she turned toward the flowers, not wanting him to see how much his touch affected her. "Did you stop by for something in particular?"

"Yes, actually, I did. We're having a surprise get-together for Mom's birthday Saturday. I was hoping you could ask

Doris to run the store that day and celebrate with us. Mom would love it."

She thought the sparkle in his eyes said *So would I*, but then again it could have been a trick of the light. "Us?"

"Yes, the whole family will be there except my little brother, Jake." Clint chuckled. "And I guess, technically, you could say he will be there, too. That day's game is televised."

"Your mom told me about him. It must be really cool to play major league baseball." The McFaddens were definitely a multitalented group. Elaine had told her that one of her other sons was a senator.

Jessa looked up at the McFadden standing in front of her. Maybe she was prejudiced, but she didn't think any of them could be as good as her. . .friend.

Thankfully unaware of her thoughts, Clint nodded. "This is his first year, and he doesn't get to play all the time, but it's what he's always wanted to do."

"That's exciting." She would love to spend Elaine's birthday with her and her family, but she couldn't. Not as long as her heart couldn't be trusted. "I think I'd better not butt in on a family gathering, though. Thanks for asking."

Clint nodded. "You're welcome to come if you change your mind."

"Thanks." She glanced at the clock. "Oh, no. Look at the time. I've got to get these flowers delivered."

"Want some company?"

Did she want air to breathe? "Sure."

He helped her carry the bouquets to the car. They set them carefully in the backseat. When they had the car loaded, the shop door locked, and were buckled in the car, Jessa looked at Clint. "Thanks again."

"It was really just an excuse to spend time with you."

In spite of the electricity jumping between them like a happy frog on a bed of lily pads, she laughed. "You think you're so smart. I guess you know I can't resist a man in a uniform." She nodded toward his shirt monogrammed with the words *Tri-Lake Security*.

He looked as if she'd punched him. Slowly he shook his head. "Actually, I think I'm not being smart at all right now, but I can't seem to help it."

When he didn't expound, she started the motor. They rode along without talking, stopping occasionally to deliver a bouquet. As they completed the map she'd laid out, Jessa made a few inconsequential comments about the road, the houses, and the flowers, but Clint never responded.

By the time Jessa pulled back into the flower shop parking lot shortly before six, her nerves were taut from her passenger's silence. When she shoved the gearshift into park, he looked at her as if he wanted to say something but opened the door instead.

"Elaine invited me to come for supper at seven. Are you going to be there?"

For a minute, Jessa thought he wouldn't answer.

"Not tonight. I've got some things to take care of."

☙

Clint flopped down on the bed, tucked his hands behind his head, and stared at the ceiling. He felt like a heel. He'd left Jessa sitting in the parking lot of The Flower Basket, and unless he didn't know her as well as he thought he did, she'd sat there crying after he left.

And it was his fault. He'd been leading her on. Since he'd gotten the job at Tri-Lake, he'd blocked the future from his mind. Only one career held any interest for him, and he was unable to have that one, so any mindless job would do. But

Jessa's comment about a man in uniform brought him to his senses.

What was he doing masquerading as a whole person? He used to be a man in uniform, with the courage that went with it. But instead of running through the wall of flames, he'd allowed his fellow firefighters to drag him out, and Ryan had died.

Jessa deserved far better. And the only way she would get it was with him out of the picture. Though he was drawn to her like a kid to a carnival, he had to stay away. Of course, after his moodiness today, he probably wouldn't have to worry about it.

He turned on his side and punched the pillow under his head. A pink note on the nightstand caught his eye. He sat up on the edge of the bed and grabbed the note.

Clint, I found this in a box of things and thought you might like to have it. Love, Mom.

His mother was a firm believer in privacy and usually didn't come into his apartment, but he'd asked her to let the dog out for him once a day since he was working. He looked at the nightstand to see what she'd left him.

Even if his name hadn't been engraved on the cover, he would have recognized the black leather-bound Bible immediately. His parents had given it to him the day he was baptized. As an exuberant thirteen-year-old, he'd carried it everywhere. When he'd gone off to college, he'd gotten a new one, and this copy had stayed behind.

Not such a subtle hint, Mom.

In spite of his cynicism, Clint held the Bible in his hands and rubbed his fingertips over the gold letters that spelled out his name. He opened the book that had built his burgeoning belief into what he'd thought—up until Ryan's death—was an unshakable faith.

Handwritten notes dotted the margins, and some verses had been underlined in pencil. As he flipped through, a yellow section caught his eye. Verses seven and eight in chapter one of First Peter had both been highlighted.

That the trial of your faith, being much more precious than of gold that perisheth, though it be tried with fire, might be found unto praise and honour and glory at the appearing of Jesus Christ: Whom having not seen, ye love; in whom, though now ye see him not, yet believing, ye rejoice with joy unspeakable and full of glory.

He shivered. In the side margin, written in a familiar teenage scrawl, was one thought.

When we go through the fire, we come out stronger on the other side.

The word *through* was underlined twice.

The concept had seemed so simple then.

Clint bowed his head and wept.

seventeen

"Which ribbon looks best?" Doris held two shades of yellow ribbon next to the arrangement she was working on.

"Definitely that one." Jessa pointed to the deeper color.

"I agree. It kind of gives it an autumn feeling but not too much." Doris neatly tied the bow. "It's hard to believe it's fall. And it seems like we're getting busier every day."

"It does, doesn't it? I was afraid we'd lose a lot of business from the wilted flowers fiasco, but I think we ended up gaining goodwill." Jessa snipped the ends off the flowers before she put them in the vase. "I really appreciated you and Seth pitching in."

"No problem. You know, it's funny how things work out. I thought about buying this place when I found out Ruby was selling."

Jessa's hand stilled. She'd never told Doris that she'd overheard the conversation about her possibly buying the shop.

"I left it up to God to work out the financing, and He's much wiser than I am." Doris touched the bow one more time and set the finished product to one side.

"What do you mean?"

"He knew I wasn't interested in actually owning the business, but I just loved my job so much I didn't want to lose it."

"Really?" Jessa had to admit she was relieved that her new friend and trusted coworker wasn't harboring feelings of resentment.

"Yep. I didn't get financing, but I didn't need it. I got to keep doing what I want without the hassle of being the owner." She nodded to Jessa. "And I really appreciate it."

"Oh, Doris. I don't know what I'd do without you."

The phone rang. Jessa reached for it. "We'll have to adjourn this meeting of the mutual admiration society until later."

Doris chuckled.

"Flower Basket. This is Jessa. May I help you?"

"Get out."

The familiar scratchy voice sent chills down her spine.

"Who is this?"

For a split second, Jessa heard something in the background. A woman's voice maybe; she couldn't be sure. The phone went dead, and a dial tone buzzed in her ear.

Doris frowned. "What's wrong?"

Jessa still held the phone in her hand. "I don't know. I guess it was just a crank call."

"Maybe it was a wrong number," Doris said.

"No." Jessa shook her head. "This person has called before."

"What did they say?"

"Well, last time they said, 'You don't belong there,' but this time they said, 'Get out.'" Jessa hated the quiver in her voice.

"Well, that's bizarre. Was it a woman or a man?"

"I couldn't tell. This time at the end of the call, I thought I heard a woman's voice in the background. But it could have been the television."

Doris put her arm around Jessa. "Honey, why don't you sit down for a few minutes?"

"No, I—"

The phone rang again, and they both stared at it.

"Well, it is a business," Jessa said with a nervous laugh. Doris motioned toward herself, but Jessa shook her head and picked up the phone.

"Flower Basket. This is Jessa. May I help you?"

"Hi."

"Clint, hi." Jessa knew he probably thought she was crazy for sounding so relieved, considering they'd parted on less than amiable terms the other night.

"I wanted to come by the shop and talk to you, but I had to work through lunch today. Listen, I owe you a big apology for the other night."

Jessa's heart thudded in her chest.

"And several times before, actually." He chuckled grimly. "As Seth would say, I've got issues. But I promise I'm working through them. So, will you forgive me?"

"Consider it forgotten, Clint." Jessa fiddled with the phone line. "Speaking of Seth, he says you two are regular fishing buddies now."

"Yes, the fish start jumping out on the banks when they see us coming."

"That must make for poor fishing."

"True, I guess it would. I better quit telling that fish story, huh?"

"Probably so."

"Remember me telling you we're all getting together for Mom's birthday this weekend?"

"Yes." She appreciated the apology, but she had *issues* of her own she'd do well to remember.

"Well, the invitation is still open."

"Thanks, Clint, but—"

"But, even if you can't come, I want to order some flowers for Mom."

"Okay." She chided herself for wishing he hadn't given up so easily. "What did you have in mind?" She picked up a pen and the order pad. Arranging flowers for Elaine would be a pleasure.

"Something really unusual."

"Um-hum. In what way?"

He laughed. "Well, let's see. . . . She's had some really odd ones over the years. You might say it's almost a competition between her kids."

"Uh-oh. Are you trying to tell me you had an ulterior motive for rescuing a florist?"

"Now you're getting the picture."

"So I take it you want me to figure something out on my own."

"Yes, that would be perfect. When can I pick it up?"

"What time will everyone be arriving?"

"Around noon."

"Then why don't I take it to my house about eleven, and you can pick it up there?"

"Can you leave the shop?"

"Yeah, I'll work it out."

"Okay, thanks, Jessa. I can't wait to see what you come up with.

Me, either.

She hung up the phone and filled Doris in on the situation.

Doris picked up the latest flower arrangement book. "Maybe this will give you some ideas." She slid it across to Jessa. "By the way, any Saturday you want me to work, just let me know. Between now and Christmas, I can use the extra hours."

"Well, if it's okay with you then, will you fill in for me this Saturday?"

"I'd love to."

"Great. I'm not going, but I would like to make Elaine a bouquet from myself and drop it off for her. I'll be here early Saturday morning working on my and Clint's bouquets."

Two hours later, the phone rang. Doris answered, then

handed the phone to Jessa.

"This is Jessa. May I help you?" Some people asked to speak to the owner every time.

"Jessa, this is Megan McFadden, Elaine's daughter-in-law." The woman's voice was soft and melodious. "I know you don't know me, but I need to ask a favor."

"What can I do for you?"

"Clint may have told you Elaine loves unusual bouquets. . ."

"Yes, he mentioned it."

"Well, it's so hard to transport a fresh bouquet, and I wondered if I could order one from you."

"That would be great. What did you have in mind?"

"Oh."

Jessa could hear a child whispering in the background. Something about a rascal being in a deep hole.

"Do you think you could just pick something unusual that she would like?" Megan's smooth voice had taken on a slightly frantic edge.

"Sure. Would you like to pick it up at my house next door around 11:00?"

"That would be perfect. Thanks so much. Oh, and Jessa?"

"Yes?"

"We would love for you to join us. Elaine loves you, and she'll be disappointed if you're right next door and not there with us."

"Thanks so much for asking. I'll think about it."

How could she not think about it? Now she had not one, but two, very unusual bouquets to dream up by Saturday. Three, if she counted her own.

❧

After Rapscallion's bedtime walk, Clint started back up to his apartment. He paused for a moment at the bottom step and looked up at the sky. The guard light was out for some reason, and the stars were so numerous it took his breath away.

Clint walked to the backyard and onto the long dock that jutted out into the lake. At the end, he sat down and soaked in the peaceful stillness of the night.

Oh, Lord, he started automatically. *Thank You for the beauty of Your creation.* He'd been praising God since he was knee high to a grasshopper.

He heard footsteps behind him on the dock. Clint looked up. His dad nodded. "Son, am I interrupting?"

"No."

"May I sit down?"

"Sure." With the puppy in his lap, Clint scooted over to one side so his dad could sit beside him.

"It's beautiful, isn't it?" his dad asked.

Clint nodded.

"Your mom thinks you're angry at God. Is that right?"

Clint nodded again. He could imagine what his dad would have to say about that.

"I can't say that I blame you." Jeb leaned back on the palms of his hands. "Sure does seem like He gave you a rough deal."

Clint didn't say anything, suddenly feeling like he was walking through a pleasant looking field sown with land mines.

"I can just imagine how bitter Becky is. He was your best friend, but he was her husband. She must be burning up inside."

Clint just stared at the grain in the wood that reflected the moonlight.

"She's probably mad at you, too, isn't she?"

"No!" Clint didn't mean to explode, but his dad didn't seem to understand that this wasn't a case of his brother hurting his feelings or swiping his last piece of gum. Some things couldn't be fixed by country wisdom. "You know she's not mad at me." He lowered his voice. "She doesn't have to be. I can do that just fine myself. I don't understand why God would let Ryan die. Why didn't He use me to save him? I was right there."

"You can search for the rest of your years and never find the answer to that, Clint." He held his hand up toward the black sky that sparkled with tiny diamonds. "Do you understand that? Were you there when God made it?"

"No."

"And you weren't there when a time for Ryan to die was recorded, either, right?"

"Right, but that's too simplistic, Dad."

"Is it?"

"If that's true, then prayers are nothing."

"Doesn't the Bible teach that prayer changes things?"

"Yes."

"Then prayer changes things. Does it teach that every prayer we pray will be answered in a positive way, even if it's not according to God's will?"

"No, but why would God will for Ryan to die?"

"Clint, I know one thing for sure. God didn't take Ryan to hurt you. Sin came into a perfect world, and with sin comes death. There could be innumerable reasons why Ryan died that day, and I can't even imagine them. Some of them could have to do with a hundred years from now. But I do know that one fact. God loves you."

"Thanks, Dad." He pushed to his feet. "I appreciate you coming out here. I'm sorry for worrying you and Mom." He ran his hand through his hair and thought of his newly started daily Bible readings. "Don't give up on me."

"We never could, Son." Jeb hugged him quickly. "Goodnight."

As Clint watched his dad walk down the dock, he shook

his head. He remembered a time when there was no situation his dad couldn't address with his wise answers. But tonight, his answers hadn't helped.

Maybe because they fell on a closed heart, he thought with a pang of guilt.

eighteen

Jessa pulled into her driveway and grinned. She knew she should feel guilty for playing hooky, but even though cool air normally dominated the forecast this time of year, this week—hot and sunny—was a throwback. After lunch when Doris had volunteered to watch the shop for the rest of the day, Jessa had jumped at the chance to take a rare afternoon off.

She didn't know yet what she would do, but it would be something fun. . .something like kayaking. She'd need a partner for that, though, because they had to leave a vehicle at the 'getting in' point and one at the 'getting out' point. One idea down, thirty to go. Unless. . .

Her gaze flitted to the house next door. Elaine had mentioned just a few weeks ago that she'd love to go kayaking. Jessa sprinted across the backyard and ran up the steps to the patio door.

Elaine peeked out with a frown on her face, but it quickly grew to a smile. "Jessa! What are you doing home at this time of day?"

"I came to kidnap you."

"Why am I not scared?"

"I don't know. You should be, though. I want you to go kayaking with me."

Elaine's expression grew doubtful, so Jessa rephrased. "Let me put that another way. I need you to go kayaking with me."

"Need me? Why?"

Jessa explained about the finer elements of needing two vehicles.

"Oh, Jess, I'm so sorry. As you probably know. . ." Her blue eyes twinkled. "I'm having a houseful of company tomorrow. It's a *surprise*, but since they come every year for my birthday, I know to clean the house. I was just getting started."

"Are you sure you just don't want to go kayaking?" Jessa eyed the immaculate house suspiciously.

"I'm sure! I'd love to. I'll have time to sit down and visit with you this weekend, but, honestly, I've got a list as long as my arm to finish before y'all arrive. I can't possibly go." Elaine grew solemn. "But I hate to knock you out of it."

"Knock who out of what?" Jeb walked in with an armload of firewood. He saw Jessa and stopped. "Don't say a word about how early in the year it is for firewood. From the time autumn even gets within breathing distance, Elaine starts after me to carry in some wood. Just in case. Just in case what, I'd like to know. In case I get so old and decrepit before fall that I'm not able to carry any then?"

Elaine slapped her husband playfully on the shoulder. "I'll pretend you didn't say that. I know you wouldn't complain about me. Especially not with my birthday coming up." She nodded at Jessa. "Jessa wants me to go kayaking with her, and I had to tell her no. But she can't go without another driver."

"Well, that's easy enough." Jeb had yanked up the phone and was dialing before Jessa or Elaine could say a word. "Clint? Jessa's here, and she's desperately in need of a kayaking partner. I know you said you had the afternoon off—" He nodded, ignoring Jessa and Elaine's openmouthed stares. "See you in a few minutes."

Jeb hung up the phone and started for the back door again.

"He was just down the road. He'll be here shortly." The door slammed behind him before either woman could say anything.

Silence hung in the air until Elaine bit her lip. "Oh, my." Her eyes pleaded with Jessa not to be mad. "He is such a problem solver, my Jeb."

"I see that." Jessa forced herself to smile. Clint's parents couldn't possibly be aware of all that had passed between her and their son. Jeb had just been trying to be helpful. "Um, Elaine. I'm going to run home and change into some more comfortable clothes. Would you mind explaining the misunderstanding to Clint when he comes and let him know his day off is his own again to spend as he wishes?"

Elaine nodded. "Sure, honey. I'll take care of it."

Jessa gave her a hug and slipped out the back door. Jeb was at the edge of the yard, restacking the remaining firewood when she approached.

He looked up, and for a second, she saw a mischievous glint in his eye. Had his call to Clint been completely innocent? Or had he been engaging in a little old-fashioned matchmaking?

"Jeb, I need a favor."

He arched an eyebrow in a way that was so much like Clint it was scary. "What's that?"

"I have some orders for flower arrangements for Elaine's birthday. . ."

Jeb nodded.

"And I need your help. Confidentially, of course."

She outlined her idea as fast as she could, and as soon as she had his agreement, she practically ran to her house.

If she hurried, she could be gone when Clint got home. That way there would be no pity offers. She could decide a plan for the afternoon once she got on the road. Even just a drive would be nice in this weather.

She quickly changed, slipped on her sunglasses, and put her hand on the doorknob. A knock sounded at the door. She cringed, then opened it slowly. "Hi, Clint."

"You ready to go kayaking?"

"No, I've changed my mind."

He frowned, drawing his eyebrows together. "Why?"

She stared at his blue eyes. She hadn't thought that far. "Um, because. . ." Well, that wouldn't get her in the top ten if she were in a beauty contest, but maybe it would suffice for an awkward situation such as this. She brushed past him and turned back to face him. "Because I just want to go for a drive."

Clint gave her a knee-weakening grin. "I know I said I don't kayak anymore, but I'm feeling adventurous today. I've been putting in some extra hours while a couple of guys were out sick, and John gave me the afternoon off."

"That's great. I'm sure you've got better things to do than paddle down the river with me."

He shook his head. "No, not really." He jerked his thumb in the general direction of the river. "I drove by the river awhile ago, and it's beautiful today. What better way to spend one of the last days of fall than lazing down the river with a *friend*."

&

The next thirty minutes reminded Clint of a Three Stooges' film. He and Jessa managed to get the kayak down and tied to the top of her car, but not before they each had a couple of bumps on the head.

Once the kayak was secured to the car and Jessa was buckled in the driver's seat, he breathed a sigh of relief.

"Don't sigh too loud, cowboy. We have it all to do over again when we get out of the water, except then it will be on your Jeep."

Clint grinned and got into his vehicle. Partly because of all the "oops" moments, loading the kayak with Jessa had been fun. And fun was something in scarce supply these days.

He watched in amusement as her little car puttered down the highway in front of him. The kayak tied to the top was almost as big as the car, and passing motorists smiled and waved.

They drove across the big bridge that spanned Spring River, and Clint glanced down at the rolling water, then back up at the blue car in front of him. Did Jessa realize how dangerous those falls could be? He was thankful his dad had called. The thought of Jessa alone on the river terrified him.

She turned right at the stoplight. He followed her, squeezing between the vehicles parked on both sides of the road through downtown Hardy. The shops were doing a brisk afternoon business.

Jessa braked suddenly. Clint brought his Jeep to a stop, mere inches from her bumper. He shook his head as three older ladies, heedless of the fact that there was no crosswalk, hooked their arms together and strolled across the road to the shops on the other side. They all waved merrily at Jessa, and he noticed she gave them a big wave in return.

Thinking of her tender spot for Seth and Doris, he smiled. His prickly pear had a heart of mush. And if he was honest, spending an afternoon with her would be worth the risk of the falls.

A honk sounded behind him, and he realized that the three ladies and Jessa were long gone, and he was stopped in the middle of the road for no reason. Heat crept up his face as he hurried on to Hardy Beach where Jessa was waiting for him to leave the Jeep.

He grabbed his keys and locked it up, then hurried to get in the passenger side of her car.

She smiled. "What took you so long?"

"Ah, some driver wasn't paying attention," he said truthfully. His face still felt warm, but there was no point in admitting she had him daydreaming in traffic.

As she drove down Highway 63, she glanced over at him. "My guess is it wouldn't surprise you to know that I now have four orders for Elaine's birthday. All for unusual bouquets made however I think best."

"Really? Four, huh? So even Jake called?" Clint rubbed the slight stubble on his chin. "I wasn't sure he would."

"Yes, Megan called yesterday. I really think she might have told me something more specific but she had to go. There was a rascal in a deep hole."

Clint threw back his head and laughed. "Rascal is Sarah's dog."

"That explains it." Jessa smiled, her eyes on the road. "Your brother Jake phoned this morning, and then, a couple of hours later, one of your other brother's wives called. . . . I believe her name was Annalisa."

"So what are you going to do?"

"I've got some ideas. We'll see how well they work out in the morning." She smiled. "I'm on vacation today."

She turned off the highway and eased down the gravel road. When they reached the low water bridge where they would put into the water, Jessa parked. Together they maneuvered the kayak off the top of the car.

"Hey, we didn't either one get bonged in the head that time." She slid on a cap and pulled her ponytail through the back.

"Yeah, maybe we're moving beyond the Three Stooges." Clint put on his cap as well. They eased the kayak into shallow water.

"Where are your Jeep keys?"

He patted the Velcro cargo pocket of his shorts.

She shook her head. "They won't do us any good at the bottom of the river." She pulled a large green clip with her keys attached and pushed the side deftly with one thumb. "Slide them on there."

When he did, she let go, safely enclosing his keys and hers together. Then she expertly clipped the whole thing to a metal ring on the kayak.

She looked up at him with a grin. "It's called a carabiner. I call it a lifesaver. Unless we lose the kayak—which we'd better not—then we'll have our keys."

"Sounds like you're planning on us getting wet."

"Not really, but it's always a possibility. Especially when I'm not kayaking alone." Her playful smile belied the cocky words.

"Even though I didn't know what a 'caribbean-er' was, I'll try not to be too much of a liability." He shook the kayak a little and pretended to lose his balance.

Jessa just grinned. "Ready?"

"Sure."

They moved in position to get into the kayak and stared at each other. She was on the left side, and he was on the right, but instead of one being in front and one in back, they were both standing at the back, ready to take that seat.

"I ride in back."

Her tone surprised him. "I always thought the bigger person rode in the back."

She shook her head. "Nope. The person in back is the one

who steers." She looked down at the water and then back up at him as if embarrassed but determined to stick to her guns. "That's me."

He could see her reasoning. She'd obviously kayaked more than he had. But he'd floated this river from the time he was small. Even before his folks bought the lakeside house, the McFaddens had taken summer vacations here. She'd only moved from Georgia a few months ago, so she couldn't be that familiar with the rapids and falls of Spring River.

He opened his mouth, then took one more look at the firm set of her jaw. He shut his mouth. He'd invited himself along, and it was her kayak. If he wanted to steer, he should have brought his own.

He settled awkwardly into the front of the boat. They paddled easily down the open water, and Clint felt some of the tension across his shoulders relax.

"You making it okay?" Jessa asked.

"Yep. No worries." He stopped paddling. Pulling his cap over his eyes, he stretched out his legs in front of him, crossing his ankles. "This is the life."

She cleared her throat. "Hey, now. I didn't say you weren't supposed to paddle. Just that you weren't supposed to steer."

"Oh?" Pretending dismay, he eased back up straight and brought the double paddle back around crossways. "I get so confused."

He felt a slight spray of water shower down on him. "Hey! That's cold."

"Call that incentive then to stay out of the water."

Since she was sitting behind him, he couldn't see her face, but suddenly he realized he knew her well enough to hear the smile in her voice. The thought brought a smile to his own face.

As they approached the fast water, Clint saw an open vee and headed for it.

"Hey!" Jessa's voice had no smile in it this time as the back of the kayak spun around.

Before Clint knew what happened, he was facing upriver, looking at the water they'd already traversed. He paddled madly to turn around, but it was too late. They were going to ride these rapids backward. Fortunately, the tiny waves guided them gently into the calmer water, where Jessa deftly turned them.

Clint cringed. He'd automatically tried to steer at the last minute. "Sorry."

"That's okay."

They moved in silence through the long hole of deep water, paddles slicing the surface in sync. It was easy to work together as long as there was no danger.

On the next "baby" rapids, as Jake had always called them, Clint instinctively steered, then stopped quickly, hoping she didn't notice.

"Do you know how to swim?" Jessa asked.

"Sure, I've been swimming since I was old enough to walk. Why?" He felt sure she wasn't looking for reassurance that he could save her. Besides the fact that he'd yet to find anything she wasn't good at, they both had on zip-up life jackets.

"You just seem a little tense."

"I'm fine."

By the time they neared High Falls, known throughout the area for their unpredictable six-foot drop, Clint gritted his teeth.

The sound of rushing water drew closer until it was so loud that Clint barely heard Jessa when she spoke.

"I'm going to let you take it by yourself." She pulled over to the bank and used the paddle to nudge the front of the kayak into the marshy land. "Then you walk it back up over there. . ." She pointed to a narrow strip of shallow water to the side. "And I'll go on my own."

"What?" He sat disbelieving in the kayak while she got out and walked to the front.

Her face, usually so open and friendly, was taut. "Clint. This isn't fun."

"No, it isn't."

She pushed a loose strand of hair behind her ear and put her hands on her hips. "You don't trust me. You use your paddle to try to steer, regardless of what I'm doing in the back. And therefore, I can't trust you. And I'm not about to go down High Falls with someone I don't trust."

One thing hadn't changed about her. She still cut to the heart of the matter. Even as Clint opened his mouth to protest, he knew it was true. He climbed out of the kayak and wordlessly helped Jessa secure it to a tree. "I don't blame you."

He left her standing there and waded along beside the wooded knoll until he was almost even with the massive cascade of rushing water. As he stared at the falls, he thought back on their trip. He knew she had more experience kayaking than he did. He claimed to trust her. But he hadn't allowed himself to give up the reins. Is that what he'd been doing with God all his life? Claiming to trust Him but not wanting to give up control?

nineteen

"We'll go together."

Jessa spun around and found herself nose to nose with the most irritating man alive. The roar of the water had muted the sound of Clint's approach until he'd spoken directly into her ear.

She started to shake her head. She thought she'd been clear. The muscles in her arms ached from trying to be sure that she could steer the way they needed to go, even if Clint decided something different. She'd had enough.

"I trust you."

She raised her eyebrow skeptically.

"Completely." He held his hands up as if in surrender.

"Why the change?"

"You were right in what you said. My life has been pretty out of control lately. I've tried to compensate by being in control of other areas."

Jessa's heart flip-flopped. "I can relate to that."

"So are we going to stand here in water and talk all day or are we going to conquer High Falls together?"

A slow grin spread across her face. "Bring it on."

They resumed their previous seats, but Jessa could immediately sense the change in Clint. She backed them off from the falls a good bit so she could have room to choose the point they went over. He sat with his paddle crosswise in front of him until she got them situated.

"Ready?" she yelled.

"Ready!" he replied.

She guided the kayak over to the left-hand side, and as they reached the crest, she barely tucked them under the edge of a limb that grew straight out over the falls.

She and Clint, through unspoken agreement, raised their paddles above their heads and yelled. An ageless victory cry. She felt they'd overcome something more than the falls.

The swirling current attempted to flip them just as they leveled out, but Jessa managed to keep the kayak steady.

"Great job," Clint yelled over his shoulder.

"Now it's your turn."

They paddled to the shallow water walk-up, and together they dragged the kayak back to the top. Jessa motioned for Clint to take the back. After he was seated, she used her paddle to steady herself and got in the front.

They screamed again as they went down, and when they reached the bottom, she breathed a sigh of relief when Clint kept it upright.

For the next hour, they took turns steering as they came barreling down the falls. Finally, Jessa unzipped her life vest and tossed it on the sand. "Why don't you try it by yourself a couple of times while I sit here and soak up the sun?"

Clint nodded. He grabbed the kayak and disappeared up the hill. Jessa leaned back and watched as he came over the falls, paddle raised high in a victorious gesture. As he reached the rolling current at the bottom, she cringed. She'd forgotten to remind him about compensating for just one person in the boat. Once he realized he was tipping, he fought valiantly with his paddle, but it was too late.

She clapped her hand to her mouth and laughed as he popped up and swam for the kayak, guiding it to the shore.

"You okay?" She smiled at him, dripping on the shore.

"Yep. I was getting really hot, putting out all that energy. . ." He stopped and raised an eyebrow. "You're not buying this, are you?"

She shook her head and grinned. "Not one bit."

He took off back up the hill without another word.

She played with the pebbles on the beach while she waited for him to appear. When he came over this time, he raised his paddle above his head and yelled, then quickly brought it down before he hit the bottom. He deftly guided the kayak out of the current and over to where she waited.

"My turn."

He looked like he wanted to argue, but he nodded. "Want me to haul it up to the top for you?"

"No, thanks. I'm used to it."

"Watch that place at the bottom. It can be a little tricky."

She grinned over her shoulder. "Yeah, I noticed. I'll be careful."

❧

Clint watched anxiously as Jessa maneuvered the kayak to the top of the falls. Even though she had on a life vest and was a skilled kayaker, he couldn't help worrying. She looked so fragile.

She swooshed down the falls, an exuberant grin on her face, easily balancing at the bottom. He couldn't keep from smiling, too, as she paddled toward him. Disregarding her independent nature, he leaped to his feet and helped her drag the kayak to shore.

"I'll go one more time, then we need to head on downriver, don't you think?" She looked up at the sky.

He nodded and followed her gaze. The sky had gone from a light blue to a dark gray since they'd begun playing in the falls. "Looks like there might be a storm coming up."

"You know what? I think I'll pass on going over the falls again." She gave him a rueful grin. "You've finally found something I'm scared of."

"It looks like it's still not too close, but we should probably get going." He started to climb in the front of the kayak.

She held out her hand. "You get in the back this time. It's your turn to steer."

He looked closely at her face. "You sure?"

"Yes, Clint. Trust has to go both ways."

They hurried down the river, smoothly navigating over the swift currents and paddling energetically together through the slower water. Suddenly a flash of lightning lit up the sky in front of them. Even from behind, Clint could see Jessa flinch.

He surveyed the area along the banks. There were residences along much of the river, but this particular area didn't appear to have any. They'd be better away from the water, though. And away from the trees that lined the river.

He guided the kayak to the shore. They pulled it up on the bank and pulling together dragged it up the steep incline until they were above the flood line. Clint didn't think this shower would last long, but there was no use in taking a chance.

Using the rope attached to the front of the boat, Clint tied the craft to a tree.

"Thanks." Jessa cast a worried glance at the sky.

It couldn't have been much past midafternoon, but the sky grew darker by the second.

Jessa's white face pierced his heart. He pulled her to his side. "It's going to be okay. God will take care of us." The reassurance slipped out of its own volition as they stumbled up the hill.

They soon came to a small clearing, and Clint knew they were safer here than they would be in the woods.

Great gusts of wind whipped at their faces, and Clint's cap blew off his head. He smiled at Jessa. "That wasn't my lucky cap, in case you're wondering."

She attempted a smile, but just then another streak of lightning flashed across the sky. A few seconds later, a loud boom of thunder seemed to shake the ground.

"Jessa," Clint spoke directly into her ear as he guided her across the field, "help me look for some kind of shelter."

No sooner had he said the words than his gaze caught a small hunter's cabin nestled at the edge of the clearing a hundred feet away. He pointed it out to her, and together, they took off in a run as great fat drops of rain began to splatter down on them.

By the time they reached the door, they were soaked to the skin. Relief filled him as the knob turned under his hand. From the look of the dust inside, it hadn't been occupied in several years. There was no furniture, but it had four sturdy walls and what looked to be a solid ceiling.

Jessa shuddered. "It's a mansion," she said, as if reading his mind.

The rain pounded down on the tin roof, making a deafening noise.

Clint left Jessa sitting in the middle of the floor and stepped to the only room off the main one. A cot with two blankets sat in the middle of the otherwise bare room.

He grabbed the blankets, shook out the dust, and headed back in to Jessa. "You cold?"

She nodded, and he wrapped the blankets around her.

"I don't need both. You take one."

He was about to refuse, but the stubborn look in her eyes

made him rethink it. He wrapped the old quilt around his shoulders, grateful for the dry warmth.

They sat in silence for a few minutes, shoulders touching, listening to the rain. Lightning occasionally illuminated the dim room through the one tiny window at the front. Every time the thunder crashed, he felt Jessa jump.

"I'm sorry you're scared."

She looked up at him, and he could see tears shimmering in her green eyes. "Me, too. You must think I'm a big coward."

"No, I don't. It's kind of nice to see you're human with fears like everybody else."

She gave a small sobbing laugh. "You don't seem to have any fears."

His heart stilled in his chest. "I have plenty."

"Like what?" Her voice was disbelieving as she leaned her head on his shoulder. The rain continued to beat on the roof, showing no signs of slacking up.

He shrugged off his blanket and put his arm around her. He looked down at her. The girl of his dreams may have come at a bad time in his life, but there was no doubt that she was the one. And if that was the case, it was only fair that she know the real him.

"I'm afraid of going into a fire. That's why I waited on the doorstep that night at the cabin until you opened the door."

Jessa looked up at him with disbelief. "You waited outside? For how long?"

He shrugged. "Seconds. Maybe even milliseconds, but the point is I couldn't make my feet move. I don't know what I would have done if you hadn't opened the door."

She sat up straight and stared at him. "I do. You would have opened the door and come in to get me."

Total confidence rang in her voice. If only he could be so sure.

"I quit the fire department in Little Rock because I knew I couldn't go back into another fire."

"What happened to make you think that?" Concern was evident in her voice. He didn't want her pity. Maybe he should stop now.

"I lost a buddy in a fire."

She shook her head. "Oh, Clint, I'm so sorry. Was he a fireman?"

Clint nodded, images of Ryan's courage in fire after fire filling his mind. "The best."

"Was he a Christian?"

Clint nodded, smiling as he remembered Ryan visiting the nursing home and driving the church van. "The best."

"Sounds like the perfect combination."

"What do you mean?"

"Who better to put his life on the line for others than one who knows where he's going when he dies?"

He let her simple question soak in for a few minutes. He'd heard it said numerous times in other ways since the funeral, but this time the thought seemed like balm to his troubled heart.

"I was only a few feet away from him when he died."

"Oh, Clint. I'm sorry. Was he afraid?"

Clint shook his head. "Not really. He'd gotten trapped on the second story of a burning house. I was almost to him. . ." The tiny cabin with rain hammering the roof faded away, and he could feel the heat from the roaring flames. "There was a wall of fire between us. He kept yelling for me to go back, to leave him, but I couldn't." Tears blurred Clint's vision, but he could still see the orange glow of the fire. "He said, 'Tell Becky I love her. I'll be waiting for her and for you, too, buddy.'" He heard his friend's voice as plain as if he were right with him.

"I was yelling to him that I would find a way over to him. . ."
Clint choked on the memory and couldn't go on. Jessa slid her
warm hand into his cold one and squeezed. "I told him just to
hang tight, that I would be there. I was praying aloud, begging
God to help me." He stared up at the dirty ceiling, his heart
pounding as he relived the most terrible moment of his life. "A
couple of other guys came from behind and grabbed me to
pull me back. Just as they yanked me away, the floor to that
section gave way. Ryan tumbled down to the first story. He
broke his neck in the fall, so they said he didn't feel any pain
from the fire—" His voice caught on a sob. "I don't want to
lose anyone else whose life is in my hands."

Jessa squeezed his hand again and sat quietly for a few
minutes. When he had calmed completely, she leaned against
him. "Clint, I know you've heard a dozen platitudes since
your friend's death. And I don't want to add any more. But
when my brother died and then I got sick, my parents were
angry with God and tried to take His control for themselves.
It wasn't possible, and the trying has made them desperately
unhappy. Not to mention what it's done to me."

He felt a flare of irritation. He didn't want her pity, but he
didn't want her criticism either. He had a right to be angry at
God. "And you think I've done that?"

"I really don't know. But think about the last thing you said.
About not losing anyone else whose life is in your hands." She
spoke tenderly and without condemnation. "If you think about
it. . .our lives are in no one's hands except God's."

"I know that." Clint did know it, but knowing it and
understanding it were two different things.

twenty

Clint sat on the wooden steps and watched the sun peep over the hilltops. Streaks of orange and red splashed gently across the light blue canvas. The masterpiece unfolded in front of his eyes, changing each second.

Both exhausted, he and Jessa had talked little after they left the cabin that had served as their sanctuary in the storm. It had been almost dark when they reached Hardy Beach.

Then when he'd gotten home, the events of the day and her words in the cabin had played over and over again in his mind. He'd fallen asleep with his Bible open and slept soundly until the first hint of light peeked in his window. Without waking the dog, he'd slipped out to watch the birth of a new day.

He and Ryan used to sit out and watch the sunrise together at the station. It had looked different, of course, against the city skyline, but God's handiwork never ceased to leave them speechless.

Clint wondered what Ryan's reaction to God would have been if their roles in that fatal fire had been reversed. Would Ryan have been angry and bitter?

Suddenly, Clint remembered one particularly beautiful sunrise he and Ryan had watched at the station.

After they had sat quietly for a few minutes, soaking in the sight, Ryan broke the silence. "You know, if God takes the time to do this with an earthly sky—with all of our problems and all the sin in the world—heaven must be spectacular."

"Yeah," Clint agreed. "It boggles the mind, doesn't it?"

"Just think, man." Ryan stretched one arm toward the color-streaked sky. "Life is a big race, and heaven is at the finish line. Doesn't that make you want to run hard?"

Clint grimaced. They'd worked an all-night fire and had very little sleep. "How much harder can we run?"

"You may have a point there, buddy." Ryan tilted his face to the newborn sun and closed his eyes. "It sure makes me want to do the best I can for God, though." He jumped up and shoved Clint's cap bill down on his face. "Last one to heaven is a rotten egg."

Clint leaped to his feet and took after his friend, and in spite of their lack of sleep and physical exhaustion, they'd ended up rolling around wrestling like a couple of kids. Remembering it now, Clint chuckled, but he felt his eyes sting with tears.

A movement next door caught his attention. Jessa's blue car pulled out of her driveway and drove down the road. What could she be doing up so early?

Of course. The flowers for his mom's birthday. Jessa must be every bit as tired and sore as he was, but she had to make four bouquets before noon.

❧

"Do you always leave the door unlocked when you're here working by yourself?" Clint's voice behind her caused Jessa to jump.

She met his eyes, and the tenderness there was almost her undoing. "Well, since Doris is going to be here in less than an hour, I just didn't think to lock it back up."

He held out a box of donuts. "I know you left too early to eat breakfast, so I thought you might be getting hungry."

"Oh, Clint. Thanks. My stomach started growling about ten minutes ago." She nodded toward the wreath she'd been working on. "Let me finish this, and then I'll sit down and eat one."

He came in and leaned on the counter. When he saw the three finished projects, he whistled. "How did you manage that?"

She winked at him. "I had inside help."

"Dad?"

She nodded.

Clint picked up a little red fireman's hat off the counter. He stared at a long minute, running his thumb and finger around the brim. Then he looked up at her. "Did you decide you didn't have room for this?"

"It was in the stuff your dad left in the bag on my porch last night. But I didn't know how you'd feel about me using it in the bouquet."

"Whatever happens from this point on, it was a part of my past." He slid it across the counter toward her. "Go ahead and use it if you want to."

Relieved, she chuckled. "I needed it so badly for balance, but I didn't want to upset you."

She pulled his basket over to her and placed the fireman's hat at an angle on top of the greenery, then rearranged the yellow lab puppy figure and miniature red Jeep. Remembering a story Elaine had told about how Clint loved to bring her dandelions when he was young, she had fastened a bunch of silk flowers that strongly resembled yellow dandelions with a slender red ribbon and laid them in the basket beside the other things. A wider yellow and red ribbon jauntily graced the basket handle.

"I can't believe you made that." He shook his head, admiration shining in his eyes.

He pointed toward the navy blue basket. "That was Jake's

Little League glove and ball. I haven't seen that in years." On one side she'd arranged bright red and yellow flowers and on the other side a scruffy old glove holding a worn baseball rested on the shorter grasslike greenery. A St. Louis Cardinals pennant waved proudly beside the ball and glove.

She nodded and grinned. "You like it?"

"Of course I do. We'll have to take a picture and send it to him. He's going to love it."

"I looked online for the Cardinal's official colors. Red and blue are their primary colors, but this bright yellow is their secondary color."

He arched an eyebrow.

She shrugged. "So? I worry about detail. I didn't want to use red, white, and blue because of Holt and Megan's bouquet." She scooted Jake's arrangement over to reveal the basket of red roses, white lilies, and blue carnations. A patchwork quilt square draped over the basket at an angle. The round campaign button pinned on it proudly proclaimed *Vote McFadden for a Brighter Tomorrow*. Tucked in behind was a small paint and brush set she'd picked up at the dollar store. Elaine's refrigerator was decorated with artistic renderings from Sarah, Megan's little girl whom Holt had recently adopted.

"Did you cut up a quilt?" Clint touched the old patchwork piece.

"No, I bought that at an antique store in downtown Hardy yesterday. Apparently it was intended for a quilt years ago but never made it."

"You've worked so hard on these, Jessa. Nobody expected this." He pointed to the large straw wreath on the counter. "And what is this you're making now?"

"This is for Cade and Annalisa to give your mom." She had wrapped the wreath in a ribbon with an outdoor scene print. "Memory wreathes are the hottest thing going this year. This is my variation. I hope they're happy with it."

"They'll be thrilled." He examined each of the small dolls Jessa had fastened to the wreath with clear plastic wire. Four of the figures—one large cowboy and three smaller cowboys—were mounted on plastic horses of the same scale. Then the mom doll, with long brunette hair, cradled a baby to her chest with one arm and extended the other in a wave to the riders.

"Incredible," he said softly.

While he inspected the wreath, Jessa finished framing a snapshot with a green ribbon. Jeb had written *Cade's family* on the back of it. When she had the framed photo ready, she reached for her glue gun.

Clint stepped away from the wreath as she fastened the picture to the bottom center.

"I can't believe what you've done." The nearness of his voice told her he was looking over her shoulder. "I know I've said that already, but it's astonishing."

Startled by his close proximity, her hand trembled slightly as she glued the picture on. When she sat the glue gun down and turned around, instead of moving back, he took her in his arms.

"I did stop by to bring you breakfast, Jessa, but I came by for something else, too." He brushed back a renegade strand of hair from her eye.

"Really?" She shivered.

"Really." With his thumb, he caressed her cheek. "I wanted to thank you for listening to me in the cabin yesterday." He smiled. "I know you were a somewhat captive audience considering the storm, but you didn't have to be so attentive."

"I wish I could have said something more helpful. I'm glad

you trusted me enough to tell me."

"Do you trust me?" he asked softly.

For a second, she wondered if she might drown in the blueness of his eyes. Her breath caught in her throat. She nodded.

His kiss was tender, like the first fresh day of each new season, a kiss full of hope and beginnings. Jessa's heart slammed against her ribs.

She pulled away and motioned toward the arrangements on the counter. "Will you help me get these to the car? And then we can have a donut."

He ran his finger absently over his lips and stared at her. "Yes. But when my family goes home, you and I are going to have a long talk."

She reminded herself that fireman or no fireman, Clint would always be a protector. Before she could reply, Doris walked in the door.

twenty-one

When the doorbell rang, Jessa took one last look at the arrangements that now decorated her dining room table. She'd hoped Clint would be back from getting take-out chicken by the time his family arrived, just in case they hated her ideas. But he wouldn't ring the doorbell.

She glanced at herself in the foyer mirror and tucked back a stray hair, then opened the door. A tall, beautiful brunette stood on the porch.

"Hi! You must be Jessa." The smiling woman stuck out her hand. "I'm Annalisa McFadden."

Jessa returned her firm handshake. "Come on in." She motioned Annalisa to follow her into the dining room. Jessa knew from the second she met her that Annalisa would be gracious whatever her true feelings, but there was no faking the delight that twinkled in her brown eyes when she saw the wreath.

Like Clint had, she touched each of the figures. "Oh, Jessa. You've captured the heart of my family so perfectly. I love it!"

"Thanks."

A tap on the door reminded Jessa they'd left it open.

"Hello?" A soft voice called from the living room.

"Come on in," Jessa answered.

"Megan! Hurry! Come see this." Annalisa sat the wreath down and walked toward the living room just as a petite blond stepped through the doorway.

The two ladies hugged tightly, and then Annalisa, her arm

still linked with Megan's, motioned toward Jessa. "Jessa, this is Megan. Megan, Jessa. From the looks of that gorgeous patriotic basket on the table, I'd say y'all have met over the phone."

"Oh, Jessa! Look at it. How did you get the campaign button without Elaine knowing?" Megan's face glowed with excitement.

All the tension left Jessa. They both loved their arrangements. "I had a helper."

"Jeb?" Annalisa guessed.

Jessa nodded, but before she could reply, they were exclaiming over Jake's basket.

"Where's Clint's?" Megan asked.

"He came down to the shop this morning while I was putting them together, so he took his with him."

Jessa barely caught the pleased look that passed between Megan and Annalisa. She blushed at the memory of Clint's kiss. If they only knew. . .

"Speaking of Clint. . . ," Annalisa said casually, "he may be a little moody right now because of all he's been through, but normally he's the most even-tempered man I've ever met."

"Yeah," Megan chimed in. "And he is so good with kids. Sarah and the boys just love him."

Jessa looked from one matchmaking woman to the other. She really didn't know what to say.

Annalisa tucked her hair on top of her head with one hand and rubbed the back of her neck with the other. She burst out laughing, and Megan did too.

"We're so pitiful," Annalisa said.

"We should have practiced." Megan touched Jessa's arm. "Clint talks about you all the time. We just wanted to give him a helping hand."

Jessa grinned. "I started to say I'm sure he would appreciate it, but I'm not really sure he would. But I do."

"Whew." Annalisa let her hair fall back onto her shoulders and wiped the back of her hand dramatically across her brow. "I thought we'd blown it with you forever."

"No way." The thought of forever with Clint's family made Jessa's heart warm, but she tried to remember how hard it was to be independent when he was around to lean on.

Megan turned to Jessa. "Are you ready to go over to Jeb and Elaine's?"

"I'd better not. I fixed that bowl of fresh-cut flowers for her, and I'll bring it over later. I don't want to horn in on your family celebration."

"Oh, don't give it a thought. You're practically family." Annalisa waved her hand in the air as if dismissing Jessa's protests.

"Uh-oh, A., don't scare her off," Megan said softly.

Jessa watched in amusement as Megan and Annalisa played a combination of funny man/straight man. "Y'all are too funny."

"We really need you," Megan said, smiling. "With Annalisa's three boys and Clint, we females are outnumbered as it is."

"Oh, nice one." Annalisa patted her sister-in-law's shoulder, then cut her gaze to Jessa. "Do it for the good of womankind. . ."

Jessa bit back a giggle. She wanted to go. "I see that—unless I want to be a traitor to my gender—I have no choice but to go."

"Oh, good." Annalisa picked up her wreath. "Now, what do you want to carry?"

❧

Clint pulled into the driveway and parked beside his brothers' vehicles. He grabbed the bags containing the fried chicken and all the side orders that went with it and jumped out. As he walked toward the porch, he glanced at Jessa's house. How could he convince her to come over?

Before he could decide what to do, her door opened and Megan, Annalisa, and Jessa came out carrying the birthday flowers.

"Hey, Clint!" Annalisa called. "Come give your sisters a hand."

He sat the chicken on the table by the door and walked across the backyard.

"Um. . ." Megan murmured as he approached. "Jessa definitely isn't his sister."

Clint could feel his face growing warm.

"Oh, yeah." Annalisa balanced her wreath in one hand and gave him a one-arm hug. "Clint, for the sake of your tendency to blush, we won't go there."

"Thank you so much, Annalisa," he said dryly. He hugged Megan. "It's great to see y'all, even if you are trying to embarrass me."

"Who? Us?" they chorused.

Since he'd hugged his sisters-in-law, he reached an arm toward Jessa automatically, then turned it into an awkward wave at the last minute. "Hi."

Her wry grin and the memory of their kiss earlier only made his face hotter.

"Hi."

Annalisa nudged him. "She's the one who has her hands full."

He raised an eyebrow at Jessa. "Need some help?"

"Just this once." She handed him Jake's basket and kept the glass bowl of cut flowers.

Megan and Annalisa walked on toward his parents' house, strategically, he thought, leaving Jessa and him to walk alone. "Sneaky, aren't they?"

She nodded. "But I love them already."

"Yeah, me, too."

"Where's your basket for your mom?"

"I slipped it into the utility room and hid it in a cabinet before I went to get the chicken." He looped the bags of food over his hand as they passed the table by the door.

"So now who's sneaky?" Jessa asked.

"All's fair in love and war. . .and birthdays." Clint smiled down at her.

"I'll have to remember you said that."

Her casual words seemed to speak of a future. A future together he hadn't dared to dream of. Could he ever be whole enough for that?

⁊⁊

Sitting at the crowded table between Megan and Clint, Jessa was relieved to bow her head for grace. As the dishes were passed around, she put a small amount of each food on her plate. She was suddenly ravenous, and she realized she never had taken time to eat a donut.

When she'd first entered, the room had seemed packed with people of all sizes. She'd felt a little tense as she acknowledged each introduction with a smile, but Elaine's obvious delight with all the birthday flowers had calmed her nerves. Letting the conversation flow around her now, she relaxed and enjoyed the food as well as the stories Jeb told about the brothers when they were growing up.

"So, Jessa. . ." A big cowboy to Megan's left that she was pretty sure was Holt leaned forward and looked at her. "Have you always wanted to be a florist?"

Remembering the roller-skating carhop answer she'd given Clint to that question, she felt his gaze on her. "Since I was about eight or nine."

"What nudged you in that direction?" Cade asked from Annalisa's side.

She looked around the table at the family, all of whom seemed genuinely interested in her. The revelation of her *big* secret hadn't made Clint treat her any differently. Maybe it was time she quit hiding her past.

"For three years when I was young, I struggled with leukemia. Thankfully, I made a complete recovery, but the flowers I received during that time made my dreary world seem so much brighter. I've never forgotten that." She smiled, surprised to find her heart lighter at the easy sharing of something she'd guarded for so long. "It's my dream to be able to brighten other people's lives like that."

"Well, I think you're an expert at that," Elaine said, beaming. "I've never gotten such wonderful birthday gifts." She looked around the table. "I know I told you all how much I love them, but it seems like this time when y'all go home, I'll still have a piece of each of you with me."

The conversation moved on, but not before Clint winked at Jessa proudly. Most people would think it was because of his mom's bragging on her, but she knew he realized what a big step it had been for her to casually discuss her childhood illness.

ও

When dinner was done, to Jessa's surprise, both the men and women jumped up to clean off the table and do the dishes. Love and laughter flowed through the rooms as if they were tangible. She recognized immediately where Clint got his penchant for teasing. His whole family loved to tease, good-naturedly, of course, and no one was immune from it.

After the dishes were done and the house restored to its perpetual state of tidiness, all the clan, with the exception of the youngest members, gathered around the television to watch the baseball game.

Jessa had never been a big baseball fan, but the excitement on the McFaddens' faces converted her. At first, she whispered her questions to Clint, and he patiently answered her. By the beginning of the fourth inning, she leaped to her feet with the rest of the family when something exciting happened.

When the camera showed Jake warming up in the bull pen, the room shook with whoops of excitement. He struck his first batter out, and from then on, the men didn't sit back down, apparently preferring to stand ready to shove their exuberant fists in the air.

"Jeb." Elaine pulled on her husband's shirt. "Sit down. I can't see." She looked across the blank spot on the couch to Jessa. "Does it look to you like Jake is rubbing his shoulder a lot?"

"Oh, Mom, don't be a worrywart." Cade's words were spoken lightly.

"I suppose you're right, but you know what problems pitchers can have." Elaine smiled. "He's doing great, though, isn't he?"

"Definitely," Holt agreed.

Jessa lost her focus on the television for a minute. Why couldn't her mother worry like Elaine? A minute or two of concern, ended with a smile, instead of obsession?

Clint grabbed her hand and squeezed. She met his tender gaze and was almost positive he knew exactly what she was thinking. Their hearts were growing more closely linked every day.

≈

This Sunday morning, it was no accident that Clint slipped into the pew next to Jessa. He squeezed her hand briefly. As he released it, he noticed Annalisa on the other side of Jessa nudging Cade. His family was definitely rooting for them. That meant a lot.

As the service began, Clint forgot about his surroundings and gave himself over to worshiping God. But the first words of the preacher jarred him to the core.

"In the Old Testament, we read of Lot's wife, who was turned into a pillar of salt because God told her not to look back, but she did it anyway. What about you? Are you a pillar of salt? Have you been looking back instead of forward?"

The man in the pulpit seemed to talk directly to Clint as he hammered home the thought of how immovable a block of salt was and how the past could stop people in their tracks. "In the book of Philippians chapter three, verses thirteen and fourteen, the apostle Paul, inspired by God, admonishes us to forget what lies behind and reach toward what lies ahead. Paul tells us that he presses on toward the goal for the prize of the upward call of God in Christ Jesus."

Clint knew that none of his family would have talked to the preacher about him, and that even if they had, the preacher wouldn't prepare a sermon specifically for him, so that only left one source of this lesson. God had brought Clint to this place today to hear the truth from His own Word.

Whether I accept it or not is up to me.

twenty-two

Monday at lunch, Clint took his sandwich out to the most deserted spot on the lakeshore he could find. He'd intended to talk to Jessa on his break, but before he did, he knew there was someone else he had to work things out with.

Clint had enjoyed the weekend with his family, but part of him had still struggled with the fact that Ryan wasn't with *his* family. Ever since the sermon that God had practically written specifically for him, he'd known that he had to come to grips with the past and then move on.

He'd been thinking all night of what Ryan said right before he died. *"I'll be waiting."* And he'd remembered again that day when Ryan had yelled, *"Last one to heaven is a rotten egg."*

Without a doubt, his friend's faith had been real. And deep down, Clint knew he had been right. Ryan was waiting in heaven. Tears ran down his face as he watched the wind ripple across the water. He could almost hear Ryan teasingly accuse him of being a sore loser.

Logically, he knew that there was nothing he could have done to save Ryan. As Jessa had pointed out that day in the cabin, God was the only one who could have done that. And He had. But instead of saving the temporal life, He'd saved the eternal one. If Becky could accept her husband's death, even while she still mourned him, how could Clint do any less?

He bowed his head and felt the breeze ruffle his hair as he poured out his heart to God.

About half an hour later, he stood, his legs shaky with

relief. He hadn't realized how weighted down he'd felt with the burden he'd carried.

Thank You, God, for all You are to me.

As Clint patrolled the perimeter of the lake, he noticed the white van parked at a picnic site. According to the lettering on the side of the van, it belonged to the church where his parents attended. Members of the youth group were piling up sticks, as if preparing to start a bonfire.

He pulled into a parking place at the site. Today was a teachers' workday at the area school, and the kids were understandably exuberant at having a day off, so he hated to be a party pooper, but he'd better warn them of the wind. As he got out of the Jeep, a man he recognized from church met him.

"Hi, Clint. I'm glad you stopped by. We brought hot dogs and marshmallows, but I was wondering if it's too windy for us to start a fire today."

"I'm afraid it might be." He glanced at the kids. He hated to disappoint them, but safety had to come first. He pointed to a grate at the next picnic area. "I tell you what. Why don't you build your fire in that grate? It won't be as pretty as a bonfire, but it will be safer with the wind like it is today. And you can still have your wiener roast."

"That sounds like a fine idea." As the man turned to break the news to the group, Clint saw Seth sitting on the outskirts. The boy saw him at the same minute and jumped up. He practically ran to Clint and dragged him away from the already relocating group.

"Clint, I need to talk to you." His words ran together in nervousness. "I've been praying you'd show up. I guess Brother Joe was right. God does answer prayer."

"Hey, slow down. What's wrong, Seth?"

"It's The Flower Basket. I'm afraid something is going to happen to it."

"Like what?"

Seth ran his hand over his buzz cut and flung his arms down to his side. "I don't know." He paced back and forth. "Oh, man, I can't say."

Clint put a steadying hand on Seth's shoulder. "Why not? Who are you protecting?" Suddenly, little things that Seth had told him about his alcoholic father came rushing back to him. "Your father?"

"I've got to go."

Seth took off for the woods.

"Seth! What might happen to Jessa's shop?"

"It might burn down." The last words were tossed over Seth's shoulder as he took off through the thick trees in the general direction of town and The Flower Basket. Clint debated going after him on foot, but since Jessa was at The Flower Basket and possibly in danger, he'd have to deal with Seth later.

He jumped into his Jeep and tore down the road toward the shop. As he approached the tiny downtown district of Lakehaven, his heart seemed to take up permanent residence in his throat. He took the last corner on what felt like two wheels.

"Oh, Father. I know You've never forsaken me. Even when I thought You did, I was the one who turned away, not You. Lord, if it's Your will, keep Jessa safe. In Jesus' name. Amen."

Clint pulled the Jeep into the parking lot and ran up to the back door. The loud buzzing of the smoke alarm sent his heart plummeting to his feet. He tried the door.

Locked.

In desperation, he pounded on it with his fist, then sprinted to the bathroom window. With trembling hands, he pulled the screen off.

Lord, please help me.

A single brick lay two feet away almost buried in the ground. Clint quickly pried it loose and slammed it into the glass, then wrapped his jacket around his arm and hand so he could clear out the jagged edges. With a flip of the lock, he raised the window and hoisted himself up to the ledge.

Acrid smoke filled the bathroom, but keeping his jacket over his nose, Clint touched the closed door. It didn't feel warm, so he cautiously opened it.

Clint did a hasty search of the front of the store, but it was vacant. The smoke alarm would make it impossible to be heard, but he had to try. "Jessa!" he yelled.

When he stepped toward the back room, his eye was immediately drawn to orange flames that danced along a pile of artificial greenery on the floor. Behind the flames lay an inert figure on the floor.

A four-foot area hadn't caught yet, and Clint murmured one more prayer and headed for that spot. When he reached the figure, questions flooded his brain. Ruby Trent lay on the floor, unconscious.

What had the eighty-year-old woman been doing in the store? Where was Jessa?

He reached behind him with one hand and unlocked the back door. Then he scooped up the elderly lady tenderly in his arms and carried her out into the fresh air.

Jessa came running up from Main Street just as Seth ran up from the other direction. Ruby stirred. Clint deposited her in Seth's arms and turned to Jessa. Her freckles stood out against her white skin.

"Where's your fire extinguisher?"

"By the sink." She grabbed his arm. "Wait, Clint. Don't go back in," she cried.

"Jessa, trust God. He's with me, and this is what I do." He hurried back into the building where the flames had spread another two feet along the greenery.

He lunged for the fire extinguisher, pulled the pin, and quickly covered the flames with the calming foam. When there was no ember left, he ran back out the door and bent over, drawing in great gulps of air.

"Clint?" Jessa's voice was thick with tears. "Are you okay?"

"Yes, I'll be fine." When he said it, he realized it was true. God had given him back his dream.

Thank You.

"There's not much damage. Did you figure out how it happened? Seth couldn't have done it. He wasn't anywhere near here. And how did Ruby get in there?"

⁊ð

Jessa's mind spun with the same questions Clint was asking. But before she could get any answers, sirens wailed. The fire engine pulled in, followed immediately by the ambulance.

Clint touched Jessa's arm. "Are you okay?"

"Yes."

Jessa nodded. "We need to check on Ruby."

When they reached Ruby, EMTs were already working with her. Seth looked up at Jessa. His face was the color of paper, and his eyes held a haunted look. Jessa took his hand, but he pulled his away and shook his head.

Evelyn Trent came running into the parking lot, tears streaming down her face. "Ruby!" She looked from Seth to

Jessa and Clint. "What happened?" she cried.

Seth took a deep breath, and his Adam's apple bobbed in his throat as if it were a struggle to speak. "Miss Evelyn, you know how confused Nana got sometimes. . ."

Jessa stared at the boy who called Ruby 'Nana.' Were they related?

He continued. ". . .when she would think Jessa had stolen her shop?" To Jessa's dismay, Evelyn nodded.

Jessa looked over at Clint. This was too much. She needed his arms around her.

"Well, in the beginning, she talked me into helping her. Nothing that would really hurt anything." His eyes held unspeakable sorrow as he looked at Jessa. "Just enough to make Jessa leave and give Nana back her shop."

"But then lately she got wind of Jessa's cabin burning, and she started trying to get me to burn the shop down. She said Jessa didn't belong there."

Evelyn gasped and put her hand to her heart. Jessa instinctively steadied her lifelong friend.

"I told her no way, but she wouldn't quit about it. I didn't know what to do, so today I finally told Clint. But it was too late."

"Oh, Jessa, I'm so sorry." Tears flowed down Evelyn's face, and she squeezed Jessa's hand. "I hope you can forgive me. It was Ruby's mental confusion that made it necessary to sell the shop. I promised her I wouldn't tell anyone." She looked at her sister who was being loaded into the ambulance. "Bless her heart, when she was lucid, she knew she couldn't handle it, but then other times. . ." Her voice broke. "I suspected that day you talked about accidents, but I questioned her after you left, and she acted like she had no idea what I was talking about. . ."

Jessa nodded. "She probably didn't."

"Will you press charges?"

Jessa shook her head. "Of course not, Evelyn. I wouldn't think of it."

"We'll pay for any damages."

"Go to your sister. We can talk about that later."

Relief flooded Evelyn's face as she hurried to the ambulance.

Seth touched Jessa's arm. "I know it's no excuse, but my mom died when I was born, and my dad took to the bottle. He'd lock me out sometimes and forget, but I was afraid to tell anyone. Afraid they'd take me away." He nodded toward the ambulance. "Somehow Nana knew. She gave me a place to stay, and to save my pride, she gave me a job so I could pay my own way." Tears sparkled in his brown eyes. "A couple of years ago, Dad straightened up for the most part, and we do okay now, but I've never forgotten what Nana did for me."

"I understand, Seth." She hugged the distraught boy.

Clint patted him on the shoulder. "You go on to the hospital with Ruby and Evelyn. They need you."

Just as he turned to walk away, Jessa thought of something. "Oh, and Seth?"

"Yeah?"

"Be sure you aren't late Monday. There's going to be a lot of cleanup work to be done before you can start your deliveries again."

He grinned, and for the first time since he'd arrived on the scene, he looked sixteen instead of a very worried thirty.

Once he was gone, Jessa turned to Clint. He nodded at the fire chief. "I have to go talk to him."

"Yes, go ahead."

She stood where she was for a few minutes, then taking a

deep breath, headed into the building to inspect the damage. Dread plodded along beside her as she walked to the shop door and peeked in. To her immense relief, the physical damage appeared to be confined to the pile of artificial greenery Ruby had apparently gathered from the cabinet. The smoke would be another matter, but if Jessa tackled it right away, she wouldn't have to be closed for long.

"What do you think?" She jumped at the sound of Clint's deep voice close to her ear.

"I think I need a hug."

"That really works out." He took her in his arms and held her close. "Because I need one, too."

After a minute, he held her at arm's length to look at her, as if drinking in the sight. "Where were you when the fire started? I saw your car in the parking lot and thought. . ." He shook his head. "Where were you?"

"I was doing some flowers for a wedding, and I needed a color of ribbon I didn't have. So I ran down to the dollar store to get it."

He clutched her against his chest again, almost squeezing the air out of her.

"I left a note on the front door," she squeaked.

He put his hand to her face and gazed into her eyes. Jessa was grateful that the emergency vehicles and their occupants, as well as the concerned neighbors, had all gone. She needed a private minute with her two-time hero.

Lakehaven's only taxi—used almost exclusively for passengers flying into or out of the tiny local airport—squealed around the corner and came to a screeching halt three feet from Clint and Jessa. *Probably some too-late tourist trying to get a front-row seat at a fire,* Jessa thought.

Still folded in Clint's safe embrace, Jessa gasped. The elegantly dressed man and woman climbing out of the backseat were no gawking sightseers.

Before Jessa could say a word, the woman yanked her out of Clint's arms and hugged her tightly. "Oh, Jessa," she cried. "My poor, poor baby."

twenty-three

Jessa's nostrils burned from her mother's signature perfume, but she knew it was useless to struggle. Betsy Sykes would release her when she got good and ready and not a minute before. Over her mother's shoulder, she caught Clint's puzzled gaze.

"Randall, did you pay the taxi? We need to get this poor child home." Her mother eyed Jessa speculatively. "You do have a home, don't you? When we got the health insurance statement saying you were treated for smoke inhalation, we drove straight to the airport. The taxi driver told us there was a fire here." She stopped her tirade long enough to glance at the building. "Was there?"

"It was a minor incident. All taken care of now."

Clint raised an eyebrow, then shrugged and turned away.

Jessa started to tell him to wait so she could introduce him to her parents, but her dad grabbed her in a bone-crushing hug. "It's good to see you, Jessa girl. We were worried sick."

With her mother still clutching her wrist, Jessa cast a glance back toward the shop, where Clint was quietly closing the door. He mouthed, "It's locked," and then, "I'll see you later."

Defeated, she nodded and meekly followed her worried parents to her car. She handed her father the keys and climbed into the backseat.

In between her mother's guilt-inducing chatter, she directed her dad to her house. She instinctively glanced at the apartment above the McFaddens' garage as they pulled into her driveway. The shock in Clint's eyes when he saw how her parents treated her—how she allowed them to treat her—came flooding back. He would never return her feelings now. Defeat flooded her soul, and she allowed her mom to lead her up the sidewalk.

Using Jessa's keys, her dad unlocked the door and shepherded his "girls" inside.

"Jessa!" Her mother moaned. "Someone else's pictures are on the wall."

"Well, when my cabin burned—"

"I still can't believe you didn't tell us that."

"Jessa, we think you should move back home with us. This is not working out." Her dad winked at her. "I saw a little flower shop that would be perfect for you not far from the house."

Just as she felt the top of her head would blow off, her mother took over. . .again. "Lie down here on the sofa, dear, and let me fix us some hot tea. Randall, you can help me."

Jessa knew from experience that they would go into the kitchen and discuss "difficult Jessa" and how best to "handle" her. A few minutes later, she felt her mother's gaze on her, but she feigned sleep. It was something she'd gotten good at over the years.

How did they do it? She'd struggled so hard for the last several months to become independent. When she'd reached Arkansas, she'd vowed that no one was going to tell her what to do. And she'd stuck to it, almost to the point of sacrificing the man who'd stolen her heart. But now, twenty minutes in their presence and she was a bowl of mush.

It was a wonder she'd ever even gotten the gumption to move here in the first place. Suddenly, she remembered. It had been prayer that had gotten her here. She'd prayed and prayed and then kept her own counsel about things until the details were set in stone. She didn't tell her parents until a few hours before she left.

But now they were here. And all of the independence she'd built up over the last few months had come crashing down.

Dear God, surely I am not as worthless as I feel, because I know You gave Your Son for me. Jessa paused and thought of the last few months. With her eyes still closed, she relaxed against the warmth of her loving Father. *My newfound independence didn't come from You, did it? You don't need me to take physical risks or refuse help in order to prove I'm strong, do You?* Tears pricked against her closed eyes. *My independence comes from being made in Your image and in depending on You. Lord, I know my parents love me, but please give them the faith to let me go. In Jesus' name. Amen.*

Calm settled over Jessa, and strength flowed through her. She got up from the sofa and tapped on the kitchen door. Her parents' furtive whispers died in the air. They both smiled at her. She smiled back.

"Mom, Dad, we have to talk."

❧

Clint stared at Jessa's back door. Ever since he'd let Jessa's parents lead her away from the flower shop, he'd felt like he'd sent Mary's little lamb home with the veal salesman.

Jessa needed him now, more than when she was rock climbing, more than when she was kayaking, and even more. . .he gulped. . .than when she was parasailing. She needed him to believe in her independence—to believe in her ability and right to stand on her own two legs. Even if it meant giving her the freedom to take risks and trusting God to take care of her. He tapped on the door.

Jessa opened the door, and her grin lit up her face. "I was about to go looking for you."

"You were?" He peered over her shoulder, where he could hear her parents' voices, but he couldn't see them.

"Let's walk." She grabbed a sweater off the hook by the door. "I'll be back in a little while," she yelled toward the kitchen.

"Okay. We'll be here." The masculine reply didn't hold any hint of the overprotective father Clint had encountered at the flower shop.

He raised an eyebrow. Jessa didn't respond but slipped under his arm and started toward the swing by the lake. The deep layers of autumn leaves crunched under their feet.

When they sat close together on the swing, Jessa turned toward him. "I'm glad you're here."

For the first time since he'd known her, peace shone in her eyes. And something else he couldn't quite identify.

He took her hand. "I discovered something today."

"I did, too, but you go first."

"I figured out that I'd walk through fire for you." He gave her a rueful grin. "And for anyone else who needed me, too."

"Oh, Clint." She squeezed his hand. "I'm so glad."

"I told the chief I'd join the department. God is able to handle things just fine without my help. I'm going to concentrate on just following His plan from now on. It's amazing how much lighter I feel." He nodded toward Jessa's house. "What's the story with your parents?"

Jessa smiled. "Leaning firmly on God, I finally stood up to them with love. It's going to be hard for them, and they certainly won't change overnight, but for the first time, they understand that their overprotective attitude was accomplishing the very thing they wanted to prevent. They were losing me."

"Something that no one in his right mind would want to do."

Tears welled in her eyes. She touched his face with her hand. "I was afraid that after you saw how I was with them, you wouldn't come."

"Nothing could keep me away," he answered, leaning toward her and brushing away one tear that had broken free.

"Really?"

"Really." With a sudden joyous leap, his heart recognized the something else shining in her eyes. God had blessed him with an incredible gift. As impossible as it seemed, this gorgeous, precious, independent woman loved him as much as he loved her.

A Letter To Our Readers

Dear Reader:

In order that we might better contribute to your reading enjoyment, we would appreciate your taking a few minutes to respond to the following questions. We welcome your comments and read each form and letter we receive. When completed, please return to the following:

Fiction Editor
Heartsong Presents
PO Box 719
Uhrichsville, Ohio 44683

1. Did you enjoy reading *Through the Fire* by Christine Lynxwiler?
   ❑ Very much! I would like to see more books by this author!
   ❑ Moderately. I would have enjoyed it more if

   _____

   _____

   _____

2. Are you a member of **Heartsong Presents**? ❑ Yes ❑ No
   If no, where did you purchase this book? _____

   _____

3. How would you rate, on a scale from 1 (poor) to 5 (superior), the cover design? _____

4. On a scale from 1 (poor) to 10 (superior), please rate the following elements.

   ____ Heroine   ____ Plot
   ____ Hero   ____ Inspirational theme
   ____ Setting   ____ Secondary characters

5. These characters were special because?_____

_____

_____

6. How has this book inspired your life?_____

_____

_____

7. What settings would you like to see covered in future
   Heartsong Presents books? _____

_____

_____

8. What are some inspirational themes you would like to see
   treated in future books? _____

_____

_____

9. Would you be interested in reading other **Heartsong
   Presents** titles? ❏ Yes ❏ No

10. Please check your age range:
    ❏ Under 18   ❏ 18-24
    ❏ 25-34   ❏ 35-45
    ❏ 46-55   ❏ Over 55

Name _____

Occupation _____

Address _____

City_____ State_____ Zip_____

Sweet Treats

4 stories in 1

These four complete novels follow the culinary adventures—and misadventures—of Cynthia and three of her culinary students who want to stir up a little romance.

Four seasoned authors blend their skills in this delightful compilation: Wanda E. Brunstetter, Birdie L. Etchison, Pamela Griffin, and Tamela Hancock Murray.

Contemporary, paperback, 368 pages, 5 ³/₁₆" x 8"

❤ ❤ ❤ ❤ ❤ ❤ ❤ ❤ ❤ ❤ ❤ ❤ ❤ ❤ ❤ ❤ ❤ ❤ ❤

❤ ❤ ❤ ❤ ❤ ❤ ❤ ❤ ❤ ❤ ❤ ❤ ❤ ❤ ❤ ❤ ❤ ❤ ❤

Presents

$\mathcal{H}$EARTSONG ♥ PRESENTS

Love Stories Are Rated G!

That's for godly, gratifying, and of course, great! If you love a thrilling love story but don't appreciate the sordidness of some popular paperback romances, **Heartsong Presents** is for you. In fact, **Heartsong Presents** is the premiere inspirational romance book club featuring love stories where Christian faith is the primary ingredient in a marriage relationship.

Sign up today to receive your first set of four, never-before-published Christian romances. Send no money now; you will receive a bill with the first shipment. You may cancel at any time without obligation, and if you aren't completely satisfied with any selection, you may return the books for an immediate refund!

Imagine. . .four new romances every four weeks—two historical, two contemporary—with men and women like you who long to meet the one God has chosen as the love of their lives. . .all for the low price of $10.99 postpaid.

To join, simply complete the coupon below and mail to the address provided. **Heartsong Presents** romances are rated G for another reason: They'll arrive Godspeed!